KATRINA

Also by Josh Stricklin

Under the Wolf Tree
The King of Evil
Ridin' the Five
The Nelson House
Katrina

Short Stories
The Legend

KATRINA

Under the Wolf Tree, Book 4

By

Josh Stricklin

SILVER LEAF BOOKS

HOLLISTON, MASSACHUSETTS

KATRINA

This book is a work of fiction. Names, characters, places and incidents are products of the author's imagination or are used fictitiously. Any resemblance to actual events, locations or persons, living or deceased, is entirely coincidental.

Cover Art by Rob Williams.

First printing November 2022
10 9 8 7 6 5 4 3 2 1

ISBN (Trade Paperback) # 978-1-60975-293-4
ISBN (eBook) # 978-1-60975-294-1
LCCN # 2022948158

Silver Leaf Books, LLC
P.O. Box 6460
Holliston, MA 01746

Visit our web site at www.SilverLeafBooks.com

For Mamaw, who never stops making these better.

KATRINA

1

Remembering

Carlos opened his eyes to the Nelson House framed by the evergreens and shrouded in mist under the stars. Remembering what had happened in that house in the woods was never this easy. He often forgot what the house looked like, but he never forgot what happened there. This was the most vivid he had seen the house since that night the house took Kevin.

The Nelson House was the apotheosis of a house taken by time and maintained by the swampy Louisiana weather. The wood was warped and splintered. The windows that hadn't been boarded up had at least one layer of green algae growing on the glass. A tree had grown up through the porch and slumped over as if trying to find sunlight. The house wasn't just lifeless. It wasn't just still, or unmoving. It waited. Waited for them to come back.

The air was humid and warm on Carlos's face. He turned away from the house looking for the downtown city lights. There were none, and a chill touched his soul. Rose Colline hadn't been this dark in years. Not since the Pizza Hut moved to a more central location and the Mexican Restaurant moved in with its flashing lights and bright yellow sign that was never turned off, not even on holidays.

The woods seemed to suck the sound from the world. The only sound was the rustling leaves beneath him as he climbed to his feet. There were no crickets, no frogs, not even a late-night cicada. Carlos gaped at the warped boards that had burned down nearly twenty years ago.

I watched this burn, he thought.

A heavy metallic bang resounded from deep in the house's soul. Dust plumed like smoke from between the boards of the porch. The "NO TRESPASSING" sign clinging to the front of the door dropped and tumbled toward him.

Carlos remembered that sound. That booming, torturous clang penetrated to the bone. Carlos wanted to turn away from the house, but something held him prisoner. Nothing in this body responded now that he was on his feet. It was like he had been unplugged from his body. The machinery turned again. Carlos heard that voice. The voice of the gunslinger. It shrieked through the walls as it had when Carlos was still just a kid.

There were days when Carlos could hardly recall the sight of the Nelson House. This, though, was something entirely different than memory. He had watched the Nelson House burn down back when he still answered to Churro, and he wasn't the only one from his group of friends who checked the woods to make sure it was still a pile of burned debris. But he was standing face to face with it again.

Carlos smelled the ash and pine. His pants were damp from the water left from the storm. Another loud bang of machinery ruffled the house, shaking the dust from its outer walls. Carlos flinched away from the house. The shriek came then. A painful, pleading sound that broke Carlos's heart. Until he remembered what they had gone through that night.

He remembered seeing his sister. Not his real sister, he knew, but something wearing his sister. Talking through her, using her to warn him that what haunted the Nelson House would be waiting for them. Feeding until it was ready for them.

Eddie was chased through the house by a deranged redneck. Jess...and the camcorder. Jamie's mother. Duke and the entire school laughing at him, calling him names. How could it know those things about them? How could a ghost see into their past. How—

Because I've always been here, a voice, rumbled into his mind. *But you forgot about someone, Churro. You forgot about me.*

Carlos backed away from the house. His eyes darted wildly around for the friend he had lost all those years ago. Looking for Kevin. No movement. No Sounds. There was nothing but pines and a house held together by very little more than Carlos's memory. "Kevin?"

Kevin, the voice snapped. *You left me to rot. The five of you got to live full lives, and you buried me in this house! You burned me alive!*

"No," Carlos argued. "We burned the house down. It took you, and wouldn't let us in."

All these years you got to see movies, and listen to bands, after you left me here to ROT!

"No. We didn't leave you. We couldn't find you. Even the police couldn't find you after the fire was out."

You all got to leave. To talk about what happened to you here. What you saw.

"We looked for you, Kev."

Well, you want to know what I saw, Churro?

Carlos couldn't speak. It was as if all the thoughts colliding inside his mind were jammed in his throat—too many trying to get out at once.

Then something crashed through the door. It flopped and tumbled over itself like a fish on dry land. The door banged against the porch wall and rebounded back to its frame. The thing rested on the porch, a smoking wad of misshapen human parts.

Do you want to see what I saw? The voice shouted.

The mass of body parts tumbled down the three porch steps. Carlos thought of a morbid slinky. He recoiled from it. As it flopped and twisted toward Carlos, it snapped upright, taking the shape of his friend. It wore Kevin's football jersey, his jeans, his earring. Even the sloppy mullet was all there. Only the mullet looked like pieces had burned away. Between the mats of hair, Carlos watched the black, bleeding skin smoke. He smelled charred flesh. The thing's teeth were brown and chipped. Its eyes were white with inky black veins around the edges.

Let me show you, the thing growled.

Then, as if being yanked by the neck, Carlos lunged through the air into to the house. He shielded his face with his arms as he crashed through the door. He heard its shrapnel litter the floor. His body thumped onto a carpet. The rugs smelled dirty, like moss from a dried-up river. He lifted his face from the dusty floor. The room was pitch black. A flicker, lightning behind a mass of clouds, caught his attention, drawing his eyes to an enormous window that stretched beyond Carlos's vision. The lightning came quietly. No thunder. No sound but that of Carlos's breathing. The light sent his shadow darting across the wall with each inconsistent flicker behind the clouds.

Carlos touched the glass, not fully believing it was there until he did. Freezing pain shot through his palm. The window froze to his skin. He tried to pull his hand free, but the pain only strengthened with every effort he made. Lightning flickered again, now reaching out from behind the black swells of cloud. From the corner of his eye, Carlos saw someone moving. There were three of them, shuffling lazily toward him. The brilliant white flashed from everywhere sending the shadows in all directions, distorting the shapes and sizes of the people watching him. He pulled harder, hard enough to feel his skin splitting. He cried out in pain.

Don't hurt yourself, hon, Jess said.

She was the only thing that made sense to him in this house, just like she was all those years ago. Her voice was warm water, melting the frozen. The panic he felt subsided. The pain was nothing more than a dull numbness.

It's just cold, Eddie said. *I think he'll be fine.*

Yeah, Duke added. *Suck it up, Churro.*

Carlos chuckled relief. "Sorry. I don't know what came over me there." He turned to his wife. The flickers illuminated her face, getting images beneath different shadows with each new vein of lightning. Her skin was pale, and with each blink she looked less and less like herself. The corners of her mouth started to droop. A roach scurried across her lips.

Churro. I don't feel well, Jess said weakly. *I think there's something on my face.*

Carlos stumbled away from her, his face a picture of fear. He watched as the cockroach crawled over his wife's face.

Churro, help us. Jess reached for him with hands that were decayed.

Behind her Eddie and Duke spoke. *Help us, Churro! They're in our mouths.*

"What are?" Carlos asked, stupidly, but in his terror, there was nothing else he could say.

The bugs, Jess said with something else's voice. It was gravelly and wet. Black water drained from her mouth, and only in the flicker of lightning could he see the beetles and centipedes draining with it. Lightning flickered and he was no longer looking at his wife but a corpse. A rotten, decayed corpse. With every step it smelled deader. *The bugs are on our face, man. Help us! They're in my mouth!* the corpse said. It advanced on Carlos. Between the shuffling corpses, Carlos saw a bright light in a room.

"What the fuck, man?" Carlos said, but it was Kevin's voice.

He shoved the man away and scrambled for the light. Someone grabbed him in the dark, ripping the front of his shirt away from him. He kicked them away.

Help us! a woman cried.

Help us! There were five, maybe six, of them now.

There are bugs under our skin, man!

They followed him. Carlos could hear them beating on the window. Shouts for help and bugs filled his ears, taking over all his senses. Lightning exploded, destroying the glass. They piled into the forever hallway. Carlos ran for the light.

Bugs!

They're on me! Get them off!

Help us!

Bugs! They're in my mouth, man!

Carlos blazed down the hallway, ducking around the dead. As he sprinted for the dark, he could see them, clawing at their forearms and faces, tearing the skin from their own muscles and bones. They stabbed at themselves with syringes.

Bugs!

Help us, Churro!

Get'm off me!

Churro reached the room, slamming the door behind him. He fell back against the wood with all his weight. He recognized this room. The posters of Joe Montana, and Dan Marino. The boombox where he and Kevin had listened to metal bands. Even the wood paneling that in some places had separated from the studs. This was Kevin's room.

Thwack

Get'm off.

Carlos bolted around to the TV. Kevin's silhouette stood between Carlos and the TV. He snapped a belt. "Kev?"

Get'm off, I said.

"No," Carlos said.

You little shit. Kevin took a step forward, his eyes white and black with veins. The room smelled like a carcass. *Gotta earn your fuckin' keep.* Kev swung at him with the belt snapping him awake.

Carlos opened his eyes to the sight of a two-year-old girl, his two-year-old girl, Dominique. Her curly black hair hung in loose, springy ribbons all around her chubby face. Her eyes the color of caramel. She wore a shirt with a green whale spraying water from the top of its head. She leaned in for what Carlos assumed was a good morning kiss. He made to kiss her, and she sneezed in his face. He blew a raspberry to get the taste out of his mouth. Dominique giggled like it was the funniest thing that had ever happened. She blew a raspberry of her own.

"Good morning to you too," Carlos said.

Dominique crawled to the end of the bed.

"That was quite the romantic father/daughter moment I just witnessed." Jess said and tossed him a towel. Jess picked Dominique off the bed and stood her on her wobbly legs.

Jess had become a woman over the years. Her slender frame curved all the way to the floor. The smile lines were only starting to show at the corners of her mouth, making her look dignified rather than older. She had dyed her hair a bright cherry red, not to cover up any grays masquerading as blondes, but simply because she wanted to try it. Her skin was lightly tanned from playing outside with kids at the daycare she owned downtown. The few scars on her face from the rubble of the Nelson House she was buried under were only visible up close when she wore make up. And since Carlos was there when she got them, she never experienced making the awkward explanation of what had made them. The ones on her arms could always be cast aside with the mention of a childhood pet, but the ones on her jawline and on her cheeks under her deep blue eyes she hid behind a mask of foundation and blush.

Carlos flinched away from the direction the towel had come. Jess laughed at him. "Geez, you scared the crap out of me."

"Cwap!" Dominique began chanting. "Cwap! Cwap!"

Jess glared at him as if to say what did we just talk about?

"I could've said worse," Carlos grinned and sunk into his shoulders the way he also did after a minor slip up. Jess hid a smile of her own.

Carlos stood from the bed and went to the bathroom mirror to brush his teeth. The chubby, acned teenager had hardened into a mound of natural muscle. His job as a foreman forced that on him, but neither he nor Jess had ever complained about that. He supposed if he had a desk job, he'd still be an unhealthy couple dumbbells overweight. At least moving two by fours and spreading cement kept him active. He spat into the sink, and when he came back up, he caught a sight in the mirror that crushed him slightly. The bald spot was growing. His days of ignoring his thinning hair were numbered. His mustache was coming in very nicely though. Compromise?

Dominique waddled into the bathroom with her mother behind her. Jess said, "We found your phone, daddy."

The phone chimed a generic ringtone. Dominique held out Carlos's flip-phone in her chubby, little toddler hand. He rubbed the sleep out of his eyes and cleared his throat. "Thank you, Dom," he said and growled at her like a big, scary monster.

"Daddy," she giggled and wobbled back to her mom.

"Hello," Carlos said, making kissing gestures in her direction.

"Carlos, it's Eddie. Is Jess with you?"

"Yeah, man," Carlos said. This was a usual occurrence. Jess was always the only person Eddie could talk to directly, even after twelve years as the television meteorologist. "She's right here." Carlos mouthed "for your" and gave her the phone.

"Hey, Eddie," she said, knowing Eddie was the only person who ever called her on Carlos's phone. She had a phone of her own, but Eddie always called Carlos first. She never asked why, but she thought it was so Carlos wouldn't feel left out. Because Carlos never brought it up, she figured it was right on the nose, and that it was working.

"Jess, it's Eddie. I think he's back."

"Who's back, dear?"

"The Gunslinger."

Jess froze, the unconscious grin on her face falling to a

"I've never called Carlos by his nickname, but right before I called, I couldn't even think of his real name. Only Churro. Is that funny?"

"It is."

"I thought it would be."

"This…whatever you found," Jess said. "Is it serious?"

"I don't know. Johnny D's Sunday? I'd love to see little Dominique again."

"Yeah, we'll see you there."

2

Louisiana's Premier Chevy Dealership

Carlos stepped into the lobby of Rose Colline Chevy: Louisiana's Premier Chevy Dealership. He was welcomed with the smell of fresh leather and a brand new '06 Camaro black as night aimed straight for him. His boots squelched on the shiny floor of the dealership.

Carlos worked for the city parks and rec department. His job didn't exist when they were kids, but after that home improvement TV show fixed up a few houses and did four whole episodes in Rose Colline, the town exploded in population. It was like a free nationwide advertisement for the city. Carlos was put in charge of the team that built and maintained the few parks, both kids and dogs, across the city. He was never sure if it was the color of his skin or his legitimate experience that made him more qualified in the eyes of the redneck higher-ups, but the pay made him not care either way. Lately he'd overseen the development of a new convention center and most of his time was spent surveying areas for development, or meeting environmental scientists for land sample work. What that meant was that he was constantly caked with mud and leaves up to his shins. The sounds his boots made on the floor of the dealership made him self-conscious about the mess he would certainly make if he were to continue forward. He turned to go back outside and kick some of the mud off, but he was stopped by the twenty-years-a-smoker voice of his friend Duke Riggs.

"Churro!" Duke's hair was perfectly coiffed like a superhero action figure. He'd grown a belly over the years, and Carlos almost didn't recognize him in the polo and khaki getup he was wearing. The wrinkles had crept onto his face and made him look five, or maybe even ten, years older than he was. Carlos stopped, half from what he was seeing and half from what he was hearing. He didn't hate the nickname—he always supposed that if you managed to eat eighteen churros in one night, you had to take something with you—but he had fallen out of the habit of answering to it. He stopped himself from going outside and stomped on the welcome mat instead, leaving a mess of dried mud. "Sorry, I forgot to shake that off outside."

"Nah, it's fine," Duke said. "I'll get you a vacuum before you leave."

Duke led Carlos into the employee lounge. They sat across a coffee table from one another on matching leather couches. The floor was a shiny black tile, now speckled with red mud. Carlos felt out of place here in his dirty hunting jacket across from Duke's suit and tie.

"Should I be in here?"

"It's fine," Duke said. "I'm a few months from owning the place anyway."

"Still think it's weird, you working for a Chevy dealership after being a devout Mustang tamer all your life. Weirder than me having a kid. You don't still have one now do you?"

"A 'Stang? God, no." Duke pretends to spit. "Won't catch me dead in a pile of spare parts like that again. It's a Vette or beat feet, brother. So, what's the occasion? Usually it's a phone call or grocery store catch up. Nothing so committed as a scheduled visit. You and Jess okay?"

The tone of the room fell. The ticking of the clock over the water cooler filled the room.

"Yeah, we're fine. I guess you remember the Nelson House?" Carlos knew the answer. Duke had taken the longest to grow up, but he never missed his turn to visit Jamie. Not one.

"Fuck," Duke breathed. He concentrated on not crying. Not just because of what happened there, but also because of what happened after. "I don't care what they said happened to Kevin, and Donnie and the rest. They didn't go missing. That fuckin' house got'm."

"Eddie says he's coming back."

"Do you believe him?"

"What do you think?"

"I think if Crazy Eddie says it's coming back, then it's coming back."

Carlos reached up and traced the letters on Duke's nameplate.

"You could at least call it first before you start diddling it," Duke said. He leaned back in his chair. Carlos pulled his hand back, avoiding eye contact. "You know I can read you right? Been in sales this long, probably the only thing I can do is read people. If all you wanted was a reunion at the Funland, you could've just called. Coming here plays your hand. What is it?"

"I had a dream," Carlos said.

"Tell me about it, Dr. King," Duke tossed a Rose Colline Chevy stress ball, bounced it off a ceiling tile, and caught it.

"I saw it," Carlos said.

"Churro." Duke leaned forward dropping his smile. He reached over and put his hand on Carlos's. "Do you want me to call the police?"

"Come on, man." Carlos fidgeted with the hem of his shirt. "You know how we all saw something different when we were there. Eddie saw the redneck that burned down his house. Jess saw her uncle. You saw—"

"Yeah, I remember."

"I saw what Kevin saw."

Duke looked him up and down. "Well, what'd he see?"

"There was this time we had to deliver something from his uncle to a house down the street," Carlos said. "A video tape of something. Kevin never told me. We took a tape in an envelope and brought it to the house. The person who opened the door—well looking back I know he was a meth head—he had these blisters all over his face. He kept talking about bugs being on his face. We were told not to go in, and not to give him anything until we got an envelope back. We were supposed to leave if he tried to stiff us."

Duke watched him. The levity had drained from his body language. "Oh, fuck, dude."

"He tried to talk us into just giving it to him. He was like, 'Come on, man. Help me out.' Shit like that. Kevin acted like he was going to leave. The man grabbed us. He had this freak strength. He looked like paper and stick. Like I could have just broken him in half, but he was a rock. His grip was a vice. I thought he was going to squeeze my arm into a pulp. Kevin went toe up in his balls and he let us go. Freaked us both out."

"Jesus Christ, Churro. Why didn't you ever say anything?"

"That shit happened all the time."

"What'd you do?"

"We gave the tape back to his uncle. We told him what happened and the next thing we knew, his uncle was storming down the street," Carlos wiped his eyes. "That was one of the scariest things that ever happened to me. I imagine the same with Kevin. The gunslinger knew that. It just wants us to be scared. It showed us all the things we were afraid of."

"We knew that. Why telling me this now?"

"Because if Eddie wants to go back, it has to be something serious."

3

Fluorescents

When Jessica Flores parked her car in the lot at the Juniper Home her hands shook as though she had been sitting in a meat locker rather than her Outback. She had smoked the rest of the joint Carlos didn't finish when he came last month, but her nerves felt like they were vibrating. She prayed. She told herself that it had been four months since she had been here, surely something was different. Jess tried to remember the face of her best friend from high school, but when she did that, she could only think of Jamie had become. Visions of Jamie smashing her face against the window set in the door to her room haunted Jess. Countless nights she woke up mumbling the nonsense her friend shrieked through the walls before she was escorted away.

Who fed you?

He doesn't want to help this time!

Bring me your behind!

She got out of the car, cleaning the imperfect mascara with a wet wipe she kept in the console for Dominique. She tossed the wipe in the trashcan by the door and pressed the green button to enter the building. The intercom speaker below the button beeped.

"Appointment?"

"Number 9756, Jessica Flores for Jamie Merritt," Jess said into the microphone. An angry robotic buzz resounded, and the door clicked unlocked.

That noise sent visions of her previous visits screaming through her mind.

Who is powerful enough to bring him to this world?

The Nelson House wasn't the thing that sent Jamie over the edge, but they—Jess, Carlos, Eddie, and Duke—agreed that it was where her descent started. Losing Kevin hurt all of them, but Jamie refused to show that. Instead, she dove face first into mountains of cocaine and rivers of liquor. She had gotten pregnant at seventeen, opening the throttle of her descent. Her mother had beat her so badly that she lost the baby. The next day she was gone.

Jess remembered the day Jamie came back to Rose Colline two years later. She had come back to town with her forty-one-year-old husband. Jamie wore a flowing white dress with a daisy behind her ear. Her eyes were bloodshot. The way she talked about cleansing her history made Jess apprehensive. Jess remembered the way her eyes flashed from dark blue to bright green as her passion for "balancing the energy of her childhood offenders" with her husband hanging on every word. Jess offered her the couch to sleep on and was relieved when Jamie declined.

That night the police lights lit up the neighborhood. The

ambulances took her parents away. Jamie had been in the Juniper Home for nearly fifteen years for killing them.

Long way from home, aren't ya?

Jess walked to the metal detector and laid her purse on the conveyor belt.

Shit, she thought. *I forgot the pepper spray. They're going to take the pepper spray.*

She walked through the metal detector and the lights stayed green. The security guard waved the wand around her. It made a high-pitched whirring noise and the guard stepped aside. She waited for her purse. Another guard reached for it before it got to her and removed the pepper spray. He handed her the purse.

"This will be at the front desk," the guard said. "Name?"

"Jess Flores," she said, embarrassed.

"You can get it when you leave."

"Thanks," she flushed and continued to the corridor leading to the visitation desk.

"Good afternoon, Mrs. Flores," said the intern behind the desk. She was a wall of woman with black hair in a ponytail dangling between her shoulders. She was young. Maybe ten years younger than Jess and strong as an ox. "You're here to see Jamie, right?"

"Yes," Jess answered politely. The intern stood and Jess saw a bandage on her left forearm. "How is she today?"

"She's…" the intern said. "She's doing better than recent weeks. She's been quiet. Unfortunately, we don't have enough security on staff to escort her to the visitation area today. A lot of people have evacuated for the hurricane. If you still want to visit, you will have to go to her room."

We haven't left yet.

"That's fine," Jess said quietly, eyeing the bandage. "What's your name?"

"Sam," the intern said. "Samantha. Whichever."

"Well, thank you, Sam," Jess said. "I'll be brief. I just wanted to see how she was doing today. Maybe let her hear my voice a little before the storm."

Sam grinned. "Right this way."

Jess followed Sam to Jamie's room.

"How do you know Jamie, Mrs. Flores?"

"Jess is fine. We were best friends in high school. We've been through a lot together."

"Hopefully, her friend will be a calming presence. She's been a little skittish this week. And recently. Nothing violent for weeks so that's improvement. Would you like for me to give you some privacy?"

Jess considered this. As she turned to tell Sam that that would be fine, she saw the saw the bandage on her arm again. "If you don't mind, would you wait around? I won't be long."

"No problem."

Jess eased up to the window. She didn't knock. She only had to learn that once. She peered through the window and saw a ball of laundry in the corner of the room. "Jamie?" she said quietly. Nothing happened. She moved closer to the vent beneath the window and repeated.

The pile of clothes jerked upward. Jamie sprang to her feet and sprinted toward the window. "He feeds off their energy!"

Out of the corner of her eye, Jess felt Sam flinch away from the door. "How are you, Jamie?"

A laugh issued from the back of Jamie's throat, sending chills through Jess. The overhead fluorescents made the scars she had clawed into her own face seem twice as deep.

"There's going to be a bad storm, dear." Jess lightly touched the door. She wanted to reach through it and hold Jamie's hand. She wanted Jamie to be normal. "Eddie says things are going to get bad. I just wanted you to hear a friendly voice before it came. Remember my voice. Just if it gets bad. Be safe okay? For me."

"They's animals afoot," Jamie growled with a thick Cajun accent. She clamped her teeth together like an angry dog. The clamping noise dug into Jess's heart. Jamie screamed a wolf-like howl. "Parkway, parkway, parkway."

Jess said goodbye, and turned to Sam. "That's all. I can go. Thank you."

As she made her way back to the front desk, she could hear Jamie howling like an animal.

AAAWWWRRRROOOOOOO OW OW OOOWWWWW!

She picked up her pepper spray. The door buzzed, and she walked outside. She made it to her car before the sobs took over her.

4

Johnny D's Carnival Funland

Dominique played in the sand at the Squish Zone, the toddler playground at Johnny D's Carnival Funland. "Daddy! Daddy! Watch me jump!"

"Let me see, sweetie. Go!"

Dominique's little legs kicked up about an inch off the ground. She lost her balance and went to her hands and knees.

"Whoa, that was a big jump! You okay?"

"I'm 'kay," Dominique said. She got to her feet and dusted her little hands off on one another.

"You're a big girl?"

"I'm big girl!"

"Fuck me backwards. That's weird, Churro," Duke said. He was eating a chocolate ice cream cone from one of the food carts in the midway. "You have a fuckin' mustache."

"You're wearing khakis and a polo," Carlos said. "And I'm the weird one?"

"Can't all wear boots to work," Duke said. "Someone

has to sell them to construction workers. Wow, you really have a kid."

"We do," Jess said. "You haven't seen us in two years?"

"I'm not exactly the target audience for kids," Duke said, taking a bite out of the top scoop of his ice cream. He sat across from them on the picnic table.

"Is that right?" Jess laughed.

"Yep," Duke agreed, using a pile of napkins on his mouth. "Beside me and Churro had a work date the other day."

"That's what it was?" Carlos asked. "You're a cheap date. Can't imagine why no one has popped the question."

"Not me. Bed'm and pay their cab fare."

"Dreamy," Jess droned.

"Hello," Eddie said, plainly from the opposite end of the table from the Squish Zone. He quietly laid an old Rubik's Cube on the table.

Jess stood and hugged Eddie.

"Mustache," Eddie said, accidentally. "I'm sorry. It just came out."

"Well, have a seat, Crazy Eddie," Duke said. He was laughing so hard that he nearly dropped the ice cream cone. "Unless you got somewhere to be. I could use a good laugh. Hey, do you still name dogs when you freak out?"

"Thanks," Eddie said. He took the Rubik's Cube he always carried from his track jacket pocket. "I'm not crazy. I'm on the spectrum."

"What spectrum?" Duke asked. Jess shook her head like she did when Dominique tried to sneak a snack while she was cooking dinner.

"What are we doing here, Ed?" Carlos said.

"Tomorrow morning, Hurricane Katrina is expected to make landfall."

"Shouldn't it be raining?" Duke said.

"Not with a storm like this," Eddie said. "But I don't think that's all that's coming."

"What do you mean, Eddie?" Jess suddenly wanted to grab Dominique and hold her tightly in her lap.

"I found this…I don't really know what it is, an urban legend, I guess. It's about a soldier from the Alamo."

"What? We haven't been remembering the Alamo, so we get hit with a hurricane?"

"Shut up, Duke," Carlos said, passively.

"Keep going, dear," Jess waved him on.

"I found the story a week ago. It rained in my town. The worst storm we had ever seen. Two days later, Katrina formed. Katrina would've formed regardless, but nothing happened to our city. I'm concerned."

"You're all over the place, bud," Carlos said. "Start at the beginning."

"Okay," Eddie said. He picked up the Rubik's Cube, and started turning its sides. "There was a soldier, like I said. He and his son fought side by side at the Alamo. His son was killed and he took him to a nearby barn. The barn had been weakened in the battle and it came down on him. After the war, there was a ritual for soldiers who died in combat. They would put a coin over each eye. It was said that the coins were for the boat ride to the afterlife."

"Spooky," Duke said, biting the other side of the scoop of chocolate. It dripped between his legs and splashed dirty drops of chocolate at his feet.

"This soldier," Eddie continued. "His name was Juarez, he only had one coin. They put it on his forehead. When he died, he only had the one coin, so he couldn't afford the boat ride."

"That's a cool story," Duke said. "What's that got to do with us, Ed?"

"His soul wandered around the desert," Eddie said. "In Mexican culture, there's a history of remembering people through telling stories about them. So when people told his story, he would bring a storm to their city. He would destroy it and send one person to the next town until he got back to San Antonio. Eventually he got back. But when he got his revenge, he still wondered the desert."

"When we saw him, there was a hurricane," Jess said.

"Yeah," Duke said. "But the house fell."

"I don't think the house has anything to do with it," Eddie said. "I think whoever died in that house when it became 'The Nelson House' they had heard the story. He killed them. There was no one to tell the story and he was trapped."

"How do you know it's the same thing?" Carlos asked.

"The way he was dressed," Eddie said. He took a piece of paper out of the other pocket in his jacket. It was a printed picture of a drawing. It had a man in a black trench coat. "All black. Head to toe. But look," Eddie pointed to the pure white guns. "Those are burned into my memory. Even when I can't remember what the house looked like, I can remember those."

Duke stopped eating, and Carlos recoiled from the piece of paper like it was covered with disease.

"You remember how he held us there?" Carlos asked. "He could've just stopped our hearts. We'd all be dead."

An image of Jamie howling like an animal flashed across Jess's mind, and she wondered if that might have been better. "Eddie, you're the one who uses your brain better than all of us. Why are you convinced?"

"I did the research. Six instances of cities just wiped off the planet because of some storm. I read the story, and we got rain. He did come, but the last town that was wiped out by a storm was this Rose Colline. Only it was called Louisville Territory. A hundred years ago. Rose Colline didn't come back until the thirties."

Eddie looked up from the Rubik's Cube for the first time since he had started talking. The three of them watched him, Carlos keeping one eye on the Squish Zone. Their faces were painted with apprehension. Duke's ice cream had melted over his hand, and he hadn't seemed to have noticed. Jess put her hand on his shoulder, feeling something wanting to be said.

Eddie tapped the finished cube on the table twice. "I was there though. I know what happened last time. It's the one thing in myself that makes no sense. I can't justify anything that happened to us that night. I believe he's coming back."

"What do we do?" Jess said.

"We send him home," Eddie said. "I have some coins

from that time. My family keeps relics from all generations. I'll bring the coins."

"Well, if what you say is true," Duke said, "you can just tell him his own story and he'll kill himself."

"Katrina touches down in the morning?" Jess asked.

"Early, yes," Eddie said. "We'll have to go tonight."

"Your parents evacuated," Carlos said. "Dominique can stay with my mom. I'm sure she can stop smoking inside for a night."

"Dom," Jess called. "Come to mommy, sweetie. We're gonna to go to Abuela's house!"

"Yay! Wayway!"

"That's right! Wayway's house!" Jess scooped Dominique into her arms. "We'll meet you at the car."

"Hold the fuckin' phone," Duke said.

"Earmuffs," Carlos said.

Dominique had already began reciting, "Holy bucky fun!"

"That's right, Dommy girl," Jess crooned. "Holy fun!" She shot a thin-lipped glare at Duke and hurried to the car.

"What do we care?" Duke said. "We just evac too, let him blow the town away, and cash in on the insurance. Who cares?"

Eddie tapped the cube on the table. "Because if he's still alive, maybe Kevin is too."

"And if we can stop him, we can get Kevin back."

"What about the other thing that was in there?" Carlos asked. "The thing that..." He wanted to say the thing that looked like my sister, but he trailed off and Duke spoke up.

"Wasn't that the house itself? That was destroyed. And I don't know about y'all, but I've checked. I check every year. Dig through the briar bushes just to make sure. It's gone."

"Where do we do this?" Carlos asked.

Duke pounded the table with his fists. He let out an excited yelp. "We just stand in the street calling him out, Brando style baby."

"The Nelson House," Eddie said. "Makes just as much sense as anything else."

5

The Nelson House

Eddie tied the end of rope to the ski rack on top of the forest green Outback. Nobody questioned it this time. The clouds formed overhead just as the sun ducked below the horizon, casting a pink canvas behind the dark purple masses. Eddie led them through the brush. The branches seemed to part for them, creating a very thin path to the clearing where the Nelson House once stood.

"Shoot straight with me, Churro," Duke said. "Having a kid, how much harder is that than having a big dog?"

"It's exactly the same," Carlos said.

"You ever tie her up to a clothesline and just let her play outside all day?"

"We just let her roam the streets," Carlos said. "She brings home a stray every once in a while, and we just take it to the shelter."

"That's not true," Duke laughed.

"Look at that," Jess said. She was almost mesmerized by the sight of it.

"Of fuckin' course the Nelson House is there," Duke said as they emerged from the overgrown path as they had as teenagers. "It was gone. Why the hell's it back?"

The Nelson House stood as if on crutches. The porch groaned under the pressure of gravity. Moss reached up the side of the house like a spreading infection. The windows were caked in a green moldy substance so thick they may as well have been painted shut. Time had eaten away at the nails holding the shutters to the house's visage. They dangled like hanging bodies, waiting to be cut down. The wood had warped in some places, rotted in others. In many places they could see straight into the house between splintered panels. On the door read a sign, NO TRESSPASSING.

Carlos heard heavy machinery turning over in his mind. He shook it away, and followed Jess up to the porch. "It's not boarded up like last time."

"It wants a piece of us," Duke answered.

Jess said, "So how do we get in?" She tried the door, but as before it was locked. She sat her backpack down on the porch. She pointed to the corner of the house by the upstairs patio. "Eddie jumped up there last time. Should we do that again?"

"I'm a lot heavier than last time, too," Eddie said. "I've grown since then, but maybe sixty pounds or more."

"Between the three of us, I don't think it'd be too much of a stretch to get you up there," Carlos said. "Might even be easier."

Duke took a step back to the edge of the porch and charged toward the door. It crumbled under his force.

"Duke, what are you doing?" Jess asked.

Duke wiped off his sleeves. "What? It'll grow back. It's not like we're housekeeping here. We're trying to kill something."

Suddenly that made more sense than anything else they were doing, and the other three followed him inside.

They looked around the foyer, and everything was exactly the way they had left it.

They could see their finger trails in the dust on the railing going up the stairs. The splinters of wood lay on the floor where Carlos had tried to hammer through the wall. Even the door to the kitchen had finger trails. Eddie bent down and picked up the lighter he had brought with him the first time. It was a zippo with a Native American headdress on it. The one he had brought the first time. It was covered with nearly twenty years of dust. Their lanterns were in the corners of the room with the sleeping bags they had planned to use that night. Eddie walked up to his Star Wars bag and picked it up. It fell apart sending flakes of nylon and cotton in the air.

"He could've vacuumed," Duke said, waving the dust out of his face. "It's not like he wasn't expecting company."

Eddie walked to the fireplace where there was some usable kindling waiting to be burned. He struck the lighter. After years on its side, the fluid had leaked out onto the gear and when the flint struck, the entire lighter caught flame. Eddie flinched and dropped the lighter into the fireplace. The fluid spilled out of a crack sending fire across the wood.

"That was easy," Carlos said. "I wish I had known that

back in the day."

Eddie tapped the fireplace with the Cube.

Jess laced her fingers between his. She remembered how he had started the fire as a kid with a piece of paper and oil from the lantern. "Your trick was just as good."

"Juarez!" Duke shouted.

Jess squeezed Carlos's hand. Carlos instinctively ducked as if to avoid a projectile.

"Come on out here," Duke shouted. "Come get a piece!"

"What are you doing?" Eddie said.

"I'm calling him out," Duke said. "That's his name, right? Juarez?"

"I don't think it works like that, buddy," Carlos said, wrapping an arm around Jess. His hands were shaking.

"He'll come to us," Eddie said.

Lightning boomed all around them. Carlos and Jess had the same thought then.

I hope Dominique is okay.

6

Champion

The lights flickered at the Juniper Home. Sam looked up at the overheads. Trepidation sped her heartbeat. The sudden silence of the air condition unit was deafening. She had become so acclimated to it that the lack of ominous susurration was unnerving. She had been making her rounds, checking the patients, ensuring a calm and quiet corridor. Lightning struck again and the overheads died. Sam froze in the middle of the hallway. Her lungs refused to breathe. She was stuck out of time, static in the dark. The backup generators kicked on, bathing the corridor in orange emergency lights the color of a sunset.

Standing at the end of the hallway was a security guard. Sam screamed. It could've been a cat, or a stuffed animal, anything really that wasn't standing there when the lights went out, anything would have caused her to scream.

"Y'awright?" The security guard shouted.

"Yeah," Sam breathed. Her head floated, and her legs nearly buckled from the sudden rush of adrenaline. "You scared the hell out of me."

"I'm sorry," the guard said. He was jogging toward her. He saw that she wore scrubs and comfortable shoes, but he didn't recognize her face. "Do you work here?"

"Yeah," Sam said, fanning herself with the clipboard she carried. The air conditioner had only been out for a few moments, but she was already getting hot. "I'm the weekend intern. I've only been here since the fifteenth. I'm Samantha. Sam."

"Girl, there's a hurricane." The guard's bald head reflected the emergency lights. He had a thick beard that covered his mouth in the dark when he talked. "Where do you live?"

"Parkway," Sam said, quietly.

"Street?"

"Apartments."

"Middle of town, right? By the Pizza Hut?"

"Yeah," Sam answered.

"Get your stuff," the guard said. "You're just an intern, and you need to be home if you're going to be in town. Shouldn't have to be here. Meet me at the front desk. Sign out before the computers go completely offline. I'm taking you home."

They went down opposite sides of the wall, leaving the door to Jamie Merritt's room alone. Inside Jamie lay, contorted and slumped, in the corner across from the pad she slept on, her blue eyes gazing madly at eternity.

"Parkway," she whispered. "Ha! Tap-tap! Ha! A storm's coming."

The room filled with little chitters and whispers of nonsense.

She ran her fingernail between the two pads at the corner of the room. She glanced to the window in the door. The yellow light cast across the wall should've held her attention. Any interruption in the norm stood out to her and caused a disturbance within her, but tonight she saw the yellow light and it reminded her of a sunset. She turned back to the corner.

"Hello, child." The voice came to her from everywhere.

Jamie froze, her face an image of surprise, her eyes wide as golf balls. Her mouth an excited oval expanding to its limit. The light that reflected into the room from the window cooled from a dull yellow to a navy blue. Her head whipped around to the door. A silhouette of a head stared at her with glowing green eyes that looked down at her. She unfolded her contorted body and dragged her legs behind her like an injured dog to the door. She sprang to her feet and met the face. She lost herself in the dull green glowing circles watching her from the other side of the glass. Her fingers reached up to touch them. She wanted to know if they were real.

Jamie felt something fill her like warm running water. She breathed it in, her body trembled, and her legs went weak. Her eyes closed from the pleasure of it. And when they opened, she could see the green reflection of her own eyes on the surface of the window.

"Jamie." The voice rumbled through her body. "I need your help."

"Yes?" she said, weakly, like begging for water. She

needed this, whatever it is.

"You came to me before. With others."

"Yes."

"I want you to help me destroy them."

"My friends?"

"Your friends? They dragged you to an abandoned house, let you watch the love of your life burn to death, and locked you in a cell. They live their lives on the outside. Like nothing happened. After what you lost? Does that sound like good friends to you?"

"My friends," she growled.

"They don't come here to check on their friend."

"They don't?"

"No," the voice said. "They come here to check on their prisoner."

"No," Jamie growled. She slammed her fist into the window.

"Let me help you punish them for what they did to you."

"Punish, punish, punish," she whispered. Her eyes never left the eyes on the opposite side of the door.

"I'll let you out," the voice said. "But you have to do something for me."

"Anything," she whispered. Her body trembled with euphoria. *This is the rapture!* she told herself. Just like the master said.

"No," the voice said. "I am not God."

Jamie's face fell. The smile melted to a frown. Tears threatened to spill.

"I am *your* God. All yours."

The smile returned with vibrance.

"Will you worship me?"

She nodded vehemently. Her messy hair shook and covered her face.

"This is what I want you to do."

The images flashed through her head. Her standing over a security guard, the blood pooling around her feet. Holding Churro's head in a toilet. Cutting Duke's throat. Beating that fucking motormouth with the stupid toy he always twisted and twisted and *twisted*. Then handing that child over to her new god as her mother watched. The tears fell. An excitement rushed through her in waves. Her eyes closed, sending the view of her room into darkness again

"There," the voice said. "That's the source of your pain. The child."

She exhaled, opening her eyes. "The child?"

"Yes. Jessica put all her love into that child. And where did that leave you?"

"Here."

"Yes. Here, alone. Bring me the child. Will you do this for me?"

"Yes," she whispered, wiping her cheeks.

"Will you be my champion?"

"Yes!" Jamie shouted. Then shrieked, "Yes! Yes! Yes!"

A loud clunk reverberated around her room. The door cracked open. Jamie gasped. She approached the door with nervous apprehension. The door slowly swung open. She reached forward and pulled it open. The silhouette stood like a mountain in the doorway. The eyes watched her. The person standing in the door wore a security guard uniform. He was bald and his beard covered the bottom half of his head. She side eyed him.

"This ain't real," Jamie said.

"Do you want it to be?" the voice asked.

"Yes."

"Then it is real." The security guard handed her a box-cutter.

She took the boxcutter with trembling fingers.

"Let's begin."

Jamie opened the blade and slashed it across the security guard's throat. She watched the glow in the eyes fade and the person behind them come back. The shock entered his face as he fell to his knees. Blood poured from his beard. He fell flat, and a pool collected and spread across the floor. Jamie's glowing green eyes darted to each side of the corridor. Something pulled her to the right, and she followed that feeling. The blood on her foot made her slip as she changed directions, but nothing would stop her.

She sprinted through the halls, following the exit signs. Lightning crashed outside. She saw the faint flicker around a corner. The rain came then. She followed the light as the oceanic swell of rain on the roof flooded the building. She sprinted through the lobby, ignoring the girl at the computer and into the rain.

"Punish," she told herself.

Someone called to her from the building.

Jamie shrieked laughter. "Punish! Punish! Punish!"

She ran into the woods on bare feet.

7

Dom

Dominique wriggled on the pallet of her Wayway's living room. Her toddler hand reached out in her sleep. It latched onto something in her dreams, and she squeezed it. The little hand rested on her chest like she was holding a tiny animal. Thunder rumbled. She squirmed for a moment and settled back into sleep.

8

Y'all Came Back

"I still can't believe this is happening." Jess gaped at the living room that was one strong wind from being in shambles. She could smell the age of this place still. The dead air. The dust.

"After what happened last time, I'll believe you if you said I'm in the matrix right now." Duke dropped his backpack, sending up a cloud of dust motes.

"Last time was different though," Jess said. "We didn't know what was here. There was always doubt. Now we know what to expect. I don't know which is worse."

"You know what I never understood?" Carlos said. "No one ever believed us. Why would we lie about our friend dying?"

"Well, if y'all had it anything like I did," Duke said, "they thought you were trying to cover the fact that he ran away."

"What the hell would we do that?" Jess snapped. "He was my brother."

"Your uncle was investigated," Carlos said. "They said he was ashamed of the tapes they found. I'm sure you understand that. Even you are."

Jess folded her arms and backed down.

"We weren't exactly the richest kids," Carlos added. "None of us. Grew up in the shitty part of town. Our parents sold drugs. And…tapes. They said statistically he should've ran away before then. They thought we were trying to help him get away. All because they never found his body."

"They never found Donnie's either, the fuck?" Duke said. "Sometimes I think that's the only reason I got my job. His dad wanted to schmooze me up and get the real story. Look at me now. I wear polos." He nearly continued, saying that two meathead jocks was a small price to pay for what he benefited after they died. The thought of Jess rounding on him until he blacked out stopped him. He didn't think Churro would bother to stop her.

"I know I don't usually say things like this," Eddie said. He faced the fire and turned the sides of the Rubik's Cube. He was hunched over speaking quietly over his shoulder. He looked the same exact way he did in the eighties. "But I'm scared."

Jess sat down beside Eddie and wrapped an arm around him. He was always like a child to her. And she like a mom. Carlos and Duke joined them but giving them space. The four of them may not have spent much time all together like this in their adulthood, but some things were like riding a bike.

Thunder shook the walls. Something fell upstairs. Some

kind of rake or shovel or

Pitchfork, Carlos thought. Every muscle in him tightened in wait for the sound of a body slumping onto the floor like a hunk of meat. He thought he might go mad if that happened again.

"Usually I can think these things away," Eddie continued. Shadows are just tree branches. Bumps in the night are just air ducts adjusting to the changes in temperature. This is something else though. There's no logic behind this. It's unknown to me, and that's what scares me. This isn't real, it's something from some other existence. And I'm not strong like you are."

"That doesn't mean we don't need you, Eddie," Jess assured.

"Did y'all hear that?" Duke asked. He eyeballed the ceiling as though looking for some scripture.

"Someone's probably playing solitaire," Carlos said. He smirked at Duke.

"What?" Duke grimaced.

"That's what...that's what you said to—"

"I know, I just don't like my words being thrown in my face like that."

"I think it's your turn to go check this time."

"I think that's a bad idea," Duke said.

"Why?" Jess asked.

"Because I don't want to."

"Dude," Carlos said.

"What am I supposed to do?" Duke challenged. "I have a gun, sure. But what's that going to do to a fucking ghost?

Just going to put holes in the sheets."

"You know it's not a guy in sheets," Carlos said.

"I think that was a joke," Eddie said.

"Good job, Ed," Duke said. "You're catching on quicker than these two. Seriously what are we doing here?"

Lightning struck a tree and a branch fell on the roof.

"Sounds familiar," Duke said.

"We're waiting for him." Eddie got to his feet. The rest of them followed suit.

"I think he's here." Duke reached in the bag for his gun.

"If he holds us in place like last time," Eddie said, scanning the ceiling. "The first one who can, tell him the story. Even if you can't. You think it. Don't stop thinking it until we put these on his eyes." Eddie held out two coins.

Another bolt of lightning shot across the sky, casting a silhouette of trees.

Shadows are tree branches, Carlos thought.

"Yorkie," Eddie whispered.

"I think he's here," Duke said.

"Pitbull."

Jess laced her fingers between Carlos's.

"Staffy."

That world turned on its head.

The four of them left the floor and crashed onto the ceiling, as gravity changed direction.

Boots clunked down the stairs from the hallway.

"Husky."

The footsteps grew closer until they were in the room. The orange firelight danced across his face. He wore all black from his boots to the hat. He shook dirt off his trench coat. He pulled the coat back and put his hands on his hips, revealing the two ivory revolvers on his waist. "Y'all came back." Juarez said.

Another flash. Gravity reasserted itself and the four of them fell. And when they landed, it wasn't the unforgiving, dusty boards they landed on. It was sand.

9

I Will Provide

Jamie ran until her lungs couldn't keep up. She arrived at a clearing and stopped to catch her breath. Surrounded by woods, she realized she was lost. Her chest heaved. There were no landmarks and the more time she spent spinning around looking for one, the more lost she became. She had lost her anchor to the world, and there was no way to differentiate the trees from the other trees. She had no idea how she arrived here or from which direction. A branch fell from a tree, and Jamie whirled around to find it. The rain and dark made it impossible to see anything beyond the clearing.

There was a gap in the brush. She tried to cross but a vine of thorns raked across her eyebrow. She screamed in pain and stumbled backward. Pain surged from just beneath her ribs. A piece of broken wood had stabbed into her side. Jamie shouted in pain. Thunder drowned her out, hid her screams from the guards who chased her into the woods. She pulled the wood out of her and cried. "Punish," she said between sobs.

"Don't cry," that voice said to her.

Jamie's head whipped around, searching wildly for her god.

"Have you lost faith in me?"

"N…no," she whimpered. She climbed to her knees, her clothes and hair clung to her.

"Good. Dry your eyes, child."

Jamie wiped her nose on her soaked sleeve. "God?"

"You're hungry."

She nodded.

A copperhead snake slithered out of the brush. It watched her with black marble eyes.

"If you're hungry, I will provide—if you have faith."

"Faith. Faith. Faith."

The snake opened its mouth and coiled itself, ready to strike. It lunged forward. Jamie stepped to one side and slammed her bare foot down on the snake's head. It wriggled beneath her bloody foot. She watched it squirm.

"Eat," the voice rumbled in her head.

She used the box cutter. The snake fell still.

"The child," the voice said.

"Punish."

"Yes, punish. Bring the child to me. Worship me."

"Yes," Jamie said. Her excitement boiled.

Lightning struck behind her. A tree clearing the brush. Jamie saw the trail as if it were highlighted across her vision. She barked laughter.

"Go," the voice instructed.

Jamie walked toward the clearing, turned back to pick up the snake, and sprinted through the woods.

10

Sofi

Carlos coughed. The air was hot, and he noticed that it wasn't raining anymore before noticing anything else. He checked his mouth for blood, but his hand came away with nothing but sand. The impact of the ground shook his insides like a child shaking a piggybank. He struggled to breathe.

"What the fuck," Duke groaned. "Why am I in sand now?"

"Where are we?" Jess asked.

"Maui," Duke said, pealing himself off the ground. "This is the beach. We won the publisher's cleaning house thing."

"Clearing," Eddie said.

"Vince Vaughn is bringing a big ass check."

"No, he's not," Carlos said. "Shut up, Duke."

"He is," Duke said. "What would that guy say no to?"

"Where are we, Eddie?" Carlos asked. He scanned the scenery. There were miles of sand beyond the few wooden buildings that surrounded them. There were twelve buildings in all in rows facing each other. At one end of the buildings was a train track that led to infinity in either direction. On the other side was an eternity of desert. They were in a Western movie. He almost expected a tumbleweed to roll past him.

"I have no idea." Eddie checked his pockets. He had dropped the Rubik's Cube, but the coins remained in his pocket. A portion of his anxiety fell away.

"Yeah," Duke said, getting to his feet. "This is matrix. I'll take the blue pill!"

Eddie noticed that Duke's voice didn't carry the way it should in open space. He snapped. Even the buildings should've supplied some sort of echo, but the sound fell dead, as if they were still in the house.

"Hello?" Jess called.

"What the hell would make you think if anyone is here that they want to help?" Duke snapped.

"Duke," Carlos said, ready to fight.

Then something fell in the building behind him. A bottle. Rather than charge the door, the four of them took a step backward. Something fell again, heavy like a body. Another thump resounded, banging off the flimsy door. Dust fell from the frame. The door opened, revealing a small girl. Her skin was dead white. Her hair was matted. Her jaw hung like a broken door on its last hinge. The teeth left in her head were rotten and covered with dirt. They could see the bones in her legs. Her eyes glowed a vibrant green color.

"Oh, I don't like that," Duke announced.

"Sofi," Carlos said. He choked on a sob. He took a step

forward, but Jess held him back.

"He doesn't want to help you this time," Sofi said.

"Well, no shit," Duke said.

Sofi's arm became a black tentacle and shot out impossibly long. It wrapped around Duke's neck and lifted him in the air. Eddie looked up, frozen in terror. Carlos and Jess leapt onto the tentacle ripping it away. The skin peeled away like layers of spiderwebs of a slab of meat. Sofi roared an unearthly sound. The tentacle slammed the three onto the sand.

"Okay, that's getting old," Duke groaned.

They struggled back to their feet.

"Sofi," Carlos said. "What are you doing?"

"That's not Sofi, hon," Jess said.

"Yes. I. Am!" the monster roared. Her mouth fell open like a snake preparing to devour a deer. The eyes faded from a glowing green to a pale gray. Bats flew from the mouth. Black liquid poured out, dripping flaming ooze onto the wooden steps. The thing jerked forward.

"What the good goddamn is that?" Duke shouted. He was already backing away.

"Eddie, dear, we gotta run." Jess pulled him away from the horror that was advancing.

Tentacles dangled out of the thing's mouth. It used its long arms to swing at them. The tentacles pounded the sand, sending up clouds of dust in the night air.

"Where are you going?" it rumbled. "Do you think you can run from me?"

Duke saw a shed out of the corner of his eye. He sprinted

between the two buildings it stood behind. The rest followed. He pulled the door and whether from adrenaline or desert-weathered hinge, the door pulled off, and the shed threatened to topple. Inside there was a collection of building equipment. He snatched up a sledgehammer.

"Is that going to do anything?" Jess asked.

"It's what we got," Carlos said.

"Jess, you and Eddie hide in here," Duke propped the flimsy door up against the frame. "We'll draw her away until we can kill her."

"It," Carlos corrected. He grabbed a shovel—it was the only thing with enough reach to make him comfortable—and followed Duke back to the midway.

The thing rounded the corner. The tentacles from its mouth twitched in spastic jerks silhouetted in the shadows of the building. The moonlight drew a line between them, and Duke waited for it to come out of the shadows.

Duke pounded the sledgehammer on the sand and readied it. He shouted, "Come on, you calamari f—"

A gunshot exploded. The sound was deafening, like it went off in their heads. The thing's head disintegrated in a confusion of gore. It fell to the ground and bled out.

"Well, that helps," Duke said.

Behind the mound of gore, the gunslinger lowered his weapon.

11

Sound from the Bathroom

Isabella Rosita Lilliana Flores was a wonderful grandmother. She smoked a little pot now and again, but that was just to calm the shakes. And prevent the shakes, of course. She had also recently lost her membership to the Y for spreading a venereal disease to half the senior swim class after she had been warned. Twice.

But those weren't the things that made her a great Way-way to little Dominique Rosita Flores. No, she cared. As her only grandparent, Isabella had to love Dominique enough for four grandparents, and she did. She ordered the finest pizza the new Pizza Hut could make, every single topping Dominique could imagine. Gallons of Dr. Pepper, she'd fill the bathtub if that's how much Dominique wanted. And all the ice cream she could make room for in that precious little tummy.

Isabella used five cans of air freshener on the furniture to eliminate the skunky smell, and it almost worked. It covered it up enough to impress Carlos and Jessica, so in her mind it worked for a while. But at half past midnight, when the thunder woke her, the smell tapped into that addictive tendency, sending her searching through the hollowed-out music box Carlos's father had given her for an engagement present, in search of a lighter and some rolling paper. A little baggy of pot waited for her at the back of the bottom drawer. She collected these and walked to the living room where she had left Dom.

Isabella and Dominique had taken every soft surface in the trailer, aside from her mattress and a single pillow, and brought them into the living room. They had spent nearly an hour constructing—or in Dom's case watching and giggling—the biggest pillow castle in all the world. The secret was to use stools to anchor the couch cushion walls and blanket ceiling for minimum drooping. Castles had to be strong after all.

Pillows and cushions and blankets piled up and up forever over Dom's little pallet of blankets and sleeping bags. And at the top was her family crest—a drawing of her, her mommy and daddy, and her Wayway on a blank sheet of paper from the back of her coloring book.

Isabella watched little Dominique sleep as she rolled her joint, Dom's thumb plugged loosely in her mouth. A tear dropped from her eye for the daughter she lost so many years ago. Isabella always smoked at the back door when she played babysitter, so the muscle memory took her out the back door even though the rain pelted the tin roof loudly. She opened the door to freezing rain and immediately shut it. She turned her attention back to the castle in the living room.

"La chica es una roca," Isabella said under her breath, jealous of Dom's ability to sleep through a world war. She tiptoed to the front porch and smoked half her joint under the small awning until her feet were too cold and wet to want to stay out. She blew out the last puff of smoke she had been holding in and reentered the trailer. The door closed quietly behind her, and she heard a sound from the bathroom. She steeled herself against her fear and walked back to her side of the trailer. The most important place for her to be was between danger and the baby.

"Hello?"

Nothing. She inched into the bathroom. She turned on the light and saw nothing. She exhaled, and the smell of weed filled the room. She reached for the air freshener spray. She didn't feel the boxcutter open her throat. And she didn't see the face of the person who had used it. She just saw the dirty reflection of a hand in the mirror as a warm numbness spread through her. She hit the floor, too weak to stand. Lightning exploded from everywhere around her. She reached for the baby. The last thing she heard was a single word, repeated three times.

"Punish. Punish. Punish."

12

Hammer in the Sand

Duke looked at the mess of blood and tentacles. "That's some boffo shit right there."

Juarez lowered his gun. His glowing green eyes shown through the shadow of his hat under the bright blue moonlight. The color faded, sending his face into complete darkness.

"What is that, a magnum?" Duke dropped the head of the hammer in the sand. "I got a story you might like."

"Duke, maybe don't test him." Carlos tightened his grip on the shovel.

"Nah, it's cool," Duke took a step forward. "You can just stop me, can't you?"

"Duke, he has guns."

"That was your first trick, wasn't it?" Duke said. Juarez watched every move he made. "But we're adults now. You know, we've had to deal with what you did to us. Everyone said we were crazy and turns out one of us was. You took our friend. Our family. That followed us around all our lives. Now it's your turn. You see, there was this soldier in the battle of the Alamo. He and his son fought side by side, and his son died."

Carlos took notice that nothing was changing, especially Juarez.

"Then a then a barn fell in on him," Duke continued.

"Duke, I don't think anything is happening."

Juarez looked him up and down under the brim of his hat.

"But there was this tradition where the medics put coins over the fallen soldiers' eyes. But this soldier never got the coins. They ran out. And they only had one. So, they put it on his forehead, and he couldn't afford the boat ride to the afterlife."

Carlos started after Duke.

"So now as a way to be remembered, he follows everywhere his story is told, and comes with a storm to destroy everything in his path."

"Done?" Juarez said.

Duke raised the sledgehammer over his head.

Juarez whipped his revolver up and with deadeye accuracy, he shot a bullet through the center of Duke's eyes.

"Duke!" Carlos shrieked.

"You ain't tell it right," Juarez said. He eyed Carlos. "Where the rest?"

Carlos clamped his mouth shut and glanced at the building out of which the Sofi monster slunk.

"Don't keep things from me, mustache." Juarez leapt away toward the building.

Carlos's legs failed him, and he dropped to the sand beside Duke. "What the hell were you thinking? You let him take another one of us. How are we supposed to do this now?"

13

The View from the Shed

The view from the shed was limited to the cracks between the fallen door and the wall of the shed. Eddie and Jess watched the tentacled monstrosity fall into a puddle of its own black blood. At the sight of the gunslinger, Jess tensed up. Eddie put his hand on her arm.

"What is he doing?"

"Listen, he's telling him the story."

They watched Duke step forward, wielding the sledgehammer.

"Something's not right." Eddie said. "He should be weakening."

"How do you know?"

The sudden realization that he didn't know came over Eddie, and he fell silent.

An explosion erupted. Eddie saw Duke's head snap back, and instinctively covered Jess's mouth. She screamed into his palm. He heard Juarez tell Carlos that he didn't tell the story right and noticed the strange way he eyeballed Carlos.

"If you scream, he finds us, and that's it," Eddie whispered. A finger unconsciously tapped on her face twice. Juarez leapt away, leaving Duke on the ground. Eddie took his hand away from Jess's mouth. "I'm sorry I touched you. This is part of it. It doesn't work if he doesn't kill one of us at least once."

Jess's eye sprung open. Mayhem scrawled across her face. "What do you mean?"

"If he doesn't kill one of us, then it doesn't matter if we tell him the story. That's the point. I told y'all. And he has to destroy the people from the town who hears the story. He has to leave one, and it's going to be Carlos."

"Why him?"

"He's the only one that speaks Spanish."

"So, what are we doing? Just waiting for him to kill us?"

"That's not how this works," Eddie whispered. "If he kills us, we won't stay dead. Not really. This is his form of torture. He's forced to relive the day his son dies, so he forces people to relive their own deaths."

"So, why are we still in the shed if he doesn't actually kill us?"

"Because if we're dead when he dies, we stay dead."

Carlos shouted. It was a yelp of surprise.

"See," Eddie said.

14

It's Over

Duke's eyes sprung open. He gasped air in his lungs.

Carlos screamed, unable to stop himself. He wiped his face. "How the fuck are you alive?"

The bloody circle in Duke's forehead pinholed and disappeared. The pain in his head was brilliant and overwhelming. He weakly reached up to the back of his head. Blood-matted hair, and his fingers came away warm and soaked. "What did he do to me?"

"He shot you in the face, Duke," Carlos said. His voice sounded dumb to himself, and he stared at Duke like a new species of bug.

"That little bitch," Duke shouted. "He lied to me."

"He shot you in the face," Carlos said. "Not much of a truth to that either way."

"No, that fucker. Crazy Eddie."

"You were just dead."

"Yeah, he didn't tell me that would happen." Duke stumbled to his feet, slinging sand in all directions. He stormed in the direction of the shed. "What the fuck, Ed!"

"Duke, he's going to hear you. He'll come back and kill all of us." Carlos didn't know what that meant exactly.

Duke stormed through the door to the shed into the sand. "He killed me?" He growled with Eddie in his crosshairs.

"He has to," Eddie said, looking into the sand.

"And you *knew*?" Duke stepped to Eddie, and Jess stepped between them.

"You need to listen. There's more to it than he told us so far."

"We can beat him and walk away," Eddie said. "We just have to do it right. We have to do it his way. He won't kill you, Carlos."

"Why not?" Duke demanded.

"He's the only one of us who can speak Spanish."

"How does he know that?" Duke said. "What, because of the way he looks? I'm Mexican too."

"Clearly not enough," Carlos said. "You're too white."

"It's not based on what you look like," Eddie said. "Do you think he doesn't know?"

A bullet exploded through the wall of the shed. The shed toppled like a house of cards. The ceiling crashed onto Duke's still ringing head. He lost his balance and went down to one knee. "Someone else needs to take one for the team. I'm done."

"After last time," the soldier said in broken English. "I learned about you. I know what you fear. I don't have to kill you to torture you."

"We were kids," Carlos said. "We're not the same people

we were."

"Is that right?"

Behind them, a group of people started chanting. "Burn them all! Burn them all!"

Eddie's lip quivered as he watched the light from the torches grow from around the corner of a building. He paled with fear. This was what he saw as a child, waiting for the rednecks to come burn his home down. Not a memory, this was the real thing. His body locked up.

"Burn them all! Burn them all!"

Jess grabbed his face and looked into his eyes. "Let's go, Eddie. Carlos will handle this." She pulled him in the direction of the alley they came down. They were met with another Sofi monster. Her pale skin so pale it nearly shined in the moonlight. She screamed in surprise. She turned him away, then one of the thing's tentacle arms swung out and wrapped around her neck. It lifted her high into the air.

"*Jess!*" Carlos sprinted to her. He cocked the shovel back and swung it down onto the tentacle, cleaving it jaggedly off the monster's body.

Jess fell into the sand. Eddie knelt to help her to her feet.

Duke came screaming between them wielding the sledgehammer. He slammed it down into the monster's face, destroying it. "Ha! Maybe someone should tell a story about me."

"Where'd he go?" Carlos said, not seeing Juarez.

"I don't know. He jumped on the building, and he disappeared," Duke said.

"We have to find him, or we'll be stuck here."

"There he is!" a single voice said from the crowd. "Get him!"

The mob of rednecks chanted. The sound of their footsteps stampeded toward Eddie and the rest of them.

"Can we please hide?" Eddie begged.

"Come on," Carlos said. He sprinted past the dead thing on the ground back into the street between the rows of buildings. A gunshot rang out sending dirt flying in front of them. "That way, into a building."

They ducked inside the closest structure just as lightning struck, opening the sky and sending rain and wind into the town. The flash showed them a glimpse of the room. It was a blacksmith's shop. Tools for all kinds of jobs from carpentry to gardening hung on the walls. Hammers and spades rattled on the walls as the rumble of thunder shook the wall. Just before everything went dark, Jess saw someone standing in the corner.

"Who was that?" Jess whispered to Eddie.

"I didn't see anyone."

"Hey, who's there?" Jess demanded.

thwack

"Get'm off, I said." The sounded of her uncle's voice covered her arms in gooseflesh.

thwack

"You gotta do you part."

The static from a TV filled the room with grey light. They were in Kevin's room. He stood there like a zombie. His skin had been picked to the bones in places. His face was covered with sores. In the corner Jess saw the red light from the camcorder and her teenage self standing in the darkness behind it.

"Run!" Carlos yelled, pulling them out the door. They were back in the street running across to another building in the rain.

A gunshot rang out. The bullet hit the ground right at Duke's feet. Duke opened the door to the building and saw the hardwood floors of a gym, and the spinning lights of a disco ball circling the room. A beautiful young girl stood beneath the ball holding her hand out. "Come to me, cariño."

"No, fuck that," Duke slammed the rickety door.

Carlos lead them to the next building, Duke following with the sledgehammer still equipped. Jess looked for Juarez on top of the buildings. She heard a thump on a nearby roof followed by gunfire and the sight of Duke's head opening like a can of soup. Blood mixed with the rain. She screamed and fell back, taking Eddie to the ground with her. She saw Juarez. He was pointing the revolver at them now. She hurried to her feet. "Come on, Eddie."

The mob came into full view. Their torches lit the road through town. Eddie was frozen with fear. Sweat beaded and rolled down his face. A pitchfork soared through the air toward him. Jess yanked his pants, sliding him out of the way of the fork's trajectory. It dug into the ground, kicking up mud.

"Burn them all! Burn them all!" the mob chanted.

Carlos sprinted into what, at a glance, appeared to be the largest building in the town. He held the door for Eddie and

Jess. He checked on Duke. His friend was moving and for a moment he had decided to wait before locking the world out of the building. Then Duke sat up and a gunshot rang out, sending the top of Duke's head reeling. Carlos slammed the flimsy door on the scene, a bullet shot blasting through its center. Thunder rumbled, and the light gave them a quick view of a small theatre with three rows of benches coming from the left, right, and center of the stage. The light flooded in from two large windows behind the bar at the back of the room.

"We can't just leave him there," Jess said.

"He's not dead, right?" Carlos asked.

"No, but that mob of rednecks is still out there." Eddie tapped the wall with his knuckle.

"What do we do, Eddie?" Jess asked.

"We have to tell him the story," Eddie said quietly. "Then we have to kill him. And do it right." He tapped the pocket with the coins in them. A small *tink* sound could be heard over the pouring rain.

Something beat on the door. "Burn them all! Burn them all!"

The banging spread from the door to the walls of the building. Dust fell on them as if they were robbing a tomb and set off a trap. The chanting continued, swelling to a deafening roar. Three gun shots rang out, opening three new holes in the door. Wet splinters flew everywhere.

Juarez kicked the door in, sending it flying through the theatre.

Jess pulled Eddie to the back of the room.

Orange light washed the theatre from behind the bar.

"They're circling us," Carlos said. "Stay away from the windows."

Juarez aimed the gun at Eddie and fired, catching him under his eye. He fell limp in Jess's arms.

Jess let out a scream that chilled Carlos to his soul.

Juarez changed the aim of his revolver, deadeyeing on Jess's heart. "You really feel it in the heart," he said.

"No!" Carlos stood.

"Stop me." Juarez said.

"*Hubo un soldado. El tuvo un hijo.*"

A boom blasted from Juarez, leveling the town to a pile of broken wood. The mob of rednecks burned in their skin and turned to ash. His head jerked back. His mouth yawned open, and the green glow of his eyes brightened to a brilliant white. Carlos watched the inside of his mouth burn orange and red. Smoke bellowed from inside him and flecks of burning debris rose up from him into the pouring rain.

"*Lucharon juntos en la batalla en el Álamo,*" Carlos continued. Rain showered down. Juarez roared, the voice of some unearthly demon. "*¡El hijo murio!*"

"Eddie!" Jess shouted. An incredible relief spilled out of her, as Eddie opened his eyes. "We need you Eddie. Where are the coins?"

"*¡Y el padre busca venganza! ¡Viene con una tormenta!*"

Duke came through the rain with the sledgehammer in hand. He reared it back and swung like Sammy Sosa. Juarez hit the ground splashing in the blood and dirty water.

"*Él destruye todo a su paso.*"

Eddie weakly carried himself to the body, writhing in an otherworldly pain. Its screeches sent flames billowing from its mouth. Eddie fell to his knees. The other three surrounded him. He dug the coins out of his pockets. He placed the first one on his right eye, face up. The body twisted under his hand.

Carlos and Jess held Juarez to the ground.

Duke wrestled a revolver out of its holster. He stood at Juarez's feet and aimed the barrel at his chest.

Eddie put the other coin over the eye with an embossed horse running at full speed. facing up. Juarez roared one final demonic howl.

Duke pulled the trigger. Flames sparked up from Juarez's mouth. A burning black ooze seeped from the bullet hole. The ooze smoked and singed Juarez's clothes. The smell of burning flesh issued from the body.

The coins heated. Eddie jerked away from them. The two metal circles glowed as they reached the melting point. Jess and Carlos jerked away from the body as if touching the eye on a stovetop. Juarez wheezed heavily. Flaming ash flew from his mouth. Then the body fell silent. In an instant it was ash in the mud.

"*Ahora está en paz,*" Carlos said.

Eddie sifted through the wet ash. "The coins are gone," he said. "It's over."

The world turned on its side again. They slid across the muddy road back into the theatre. Their bodies pounded on the wood planks.

The world went black.

15

Doors

They opened their eyes one at a time. Jess sat up first. The smell of the dusty house and the fire filled her nose. Outside the sun shown so brightly that her mind almost let her believe she could smell coffee. "Is the hurricane over?"

"I guess so," Carlos said, stretching his back. "Was that real?"

"Fuck me if it wasn't," Duke said. "I just want to say it's bullshit that I got shot in the face three times."

"It hurts," Eddie said. "I have a headache."

"You fuckin' right, Ed," Duke said. He clapped Eddie on the shoulder. "Back from the dead, right buddy?" He held his fist up to Eddie, and in a shocking instant, rather than moving away from Duke. Eddie tapped his knuckles with the Rubik's Cube. "Goddamn right, buddy. We're both crazy now."

Jess reached for Carlos. He put her hand in his. "I'm just glad that's over. I want to see my girl."

"Don't we all," Carlos said. He let out a groan as he

climbed to his feet.

"Christ," Duke said. "You are definitely a middle-aged dad in the making."

"Give me a break. After all that?"

"I died three times," Duke said. "You don't get to win with me anymore."

They got to their feet and packed up their things.

Duke realized that he still carried the revolver in a belt loop of his jeans. "Hey, hey! Souvenir!"

"I don't know, man," Carlos said. "You sure you want that around you."

"Damn right, I do. What if I need it?"

"Whatever you say," Carlos agreed. He pulled Jess closer to him.

They walked to the foyer together, and Duke stopped them. He looked around. "Should we say something?"

"This isn't Family Matters, Duke," Jess said. "Let's just go."

"I mean for Kev," Duke said.

Jess's smile fell. "Maybe later. Not here."

Carlos opened the door and rather than walking onto the porch, he found himself back in the living room.

"I'm sorry," Duke said. "I guess I just woke up, because now we're in the living room again."

Carlos walked across the house and opened the front door. It led into another living room.

Duke eyed the view from this door. "Ed, open that back door."

"It's locked," Eddie said.

"Keep this door open," Duke told Carlos. "I'm going to open that door, and you'll have this door open, and then we'll be able to see through all the doors, and surely one of them will work."

"You sound like a lunatic," Carlos said.

"Just do it." Duke walked the through house again and opened the front door. It was another repeat of the house, but this time, Sofi charged at him again, her tentacles swinging madly. Duke lunged backward, ripping the gun from his belt. He dropped it. The Sofi monster entered his part of the house, slamming the door behind her. It made a gargling noise behind the tentacles on her face. Her eyes glowed a bright green color.

Duke picked up the revolver and fired it.

The shot struck the monster in the neck. The wound nearly severed her head. It took two jerky steps forward and dropped to the floor. Blood pooled around her.

"Suck my dick, little girl," Duke said.

The door fell open. On the other side, the clearing in the woods waited to usher them back home.

"Elegantly put, Duke," Carlos said.

"Now how are you so certain that that wasn't the password to get the hell out of here?"

"I really don't think it was."

"Eddie," Jess asked. "Is this over?"

"Well, the door opened," he answered. "And it's quiet. Nothing else is coming."

"We're good," Duke said. "Unless…" Duke's eyebrows raised. He waited for anything to happen. He listened for something other than the far away cry of a bird, or the frogs croaking. When nothing happened, he looked at them with a crooked smirk. "See? Nothing."

The four of them walked out of the Nelson House, greeted with the smell of pine and warm rays of the sun on their faces. They followed the rope back to the Outback and piled their stuff into the back of it. Jess backed the car out, and they left.

16

The Hotel Room

"Still a little fucked up that he killed me so many times," Duke said.

"You *were* the one that sassed him," Jess said.

"And?"

"Relentlessly," Carlos chimed in. He and Jess laughed. "I will say it took a hefty pair of onions to bring a hammer to a shootout."

"You gotta have confidence," Duke said. He propped his foot on the console between the front seat. He felt the back of his head. His hair was sticky with dried blood. "Can you believe I died? That's insane. I didn't even know it happened. I was standing there, and then I was laying there with Churro leaned over me and ugly-crying."

"I've never seen a dead body with a gunshot to the head," Carlos said. "Freaked me out."

"I thought I was about to get the mouth-to-mouth treatment."

Jess gave Carlos a look that said she wanted to get the

mouth-to-mouth treatment and slid her fingers between his. "This has followed us around for almost twenty years. We were kids when this started. I feel like we just got out of prison."

Something ran out in front of them. It was black, and its fur was patchy. It was as big as a bear but looked like an emaciated panther. The skin rippled over the ribs, and its eyes seemed to reflect as if from headlights in the dark. It was dragging an animal by its neck. Jess stood on the brake pedal and the car screeched to a halt well before the thing in the road. Jess fought the urge to put the car in reverse and floor the accelerator. She wanted to be as far from that thing as she could. It bit down on the neck of what looked like a deer. Its ripped away the meat, and its focus shifted to the car. It chewed as it watched.

"Don't move," Carlos said.

"It's not a fuckin' t-rex," Duke said, but remained as perfectly still as the rest of the car.

When the thing in the road seemed to be satisfied, it swallowed and crossed into the woods, leaving the deer carcass behind.

"What in the fuck was that?" Duke said. He watched the woods, waiting for it to return.

Jess slowly drove around the deer, and quickly sped away. Her heart pounded, and when the carcass was out of sight, she finally remembered to breathe.

"Was that a panther?" Carlos said.

"Eddie, have you ever seen one of those before?" Jess asked, into the rearview mirror.

"I suppose it could've been a sick panther," Eddie said. "Those usually inhabit swampy marshlands, and that's about ninety percent of Louisiana."

Carlos waited. "But?"

"I've never heard of one being that big. The hair looked wiry and thin. I guess it could've been in a fire, or in a bad fight. But I don't know anything that would fight something like that."

"Well, it's gone." Duke believed it, but it didn't stop him from searching the woods.

"How long are you in town, Eddie?" Jess asked, more to change the subject than anything else, but she did genuinely want to have him over for dinner before he left.

"They gave me a free night, so at least until tomorrow," Eddie said.

"How'd you get a free night?" Jess asked, falling into the ebb and flow of the conversation.

"Hurricane discount, they said."

"That makes sense," Carlos said. "Most people evacuate this time of year."

The hotel came into view, and Jess parked the Outback by Eddie's car. She helped him get his stuff out of the back. She hugged him and told him he was invited to dinner later that night. He could stay with them if he wanted, but when he turned that down, she understood.

Eddie waved and entered the hotel room. He dusted his feet off on the welcome matt.

Left, right, left, right, as always. He felt for the pewter figurine of the voodoo spirits Papa Legba and Baron Samedi his producer had given him, mistaking Native American culture for something entirely different. Eddie didn't know whether that had been an attempt at bonding or hazing, but that wasn't the kind of thing he needed to know. Eddie's relationship with the producer never changed regardless.

He had bumped the figurine on the way out of the room. He didn't bother resetting it to its very specific spot on the dresser, because that was the exact thing that his mind could latch onto when a sudden unexpected noise or vision overwhelmed his senses, converting him to a mass of shakes and gibberish on the ground. He didn't like that, and he did everything he could to prevent it from happening. Now, Eddie realigned the figurine with the corner of the dresser, an inch and quarter in and back, and opened his eyes to a dark hotel room.

He flipped the switch for the light and scanned the room.

Rottweiler

His bag lay on the floor between the air conditioner unit and the wall to his left. The bed farthest away from him was still made up the way the maids had left it. The floor was a drab mold color that looked wet and smelled faintly of a pet's potty-training accident. The door to the bathroom was closed.

Pitbull

The TV was off and the remote pointed toward the door. His laptop waited for him on the small desk in the corner. There was a pen and pad with the hotel's logo at the top sitting next to it. The phone on the side table between the two beds was black with large numbers, and the alarm clock was plugged into a standing side table lamp.

Staffy

Eddie checked his watch. The digital read out said 7:38.

Great Dane

Eddie had left his bag on the floor between the air conditioner and the wall, but when he had left it, it lay against the wall rather than perpendicular so that if the housekeeping crew did have a chance to come by the room and ignored the tag on the door, they wouldn't see it until they left, if at all. Which was why he had slept it the bed away from the door—so they wouldn't bother making up the one near the AC and finding his bag—and he had made it back up, but to his standards, which, while meticulous, didn't require him to retuck the comforter under the mattress the way the housekeeping had.

Labrador

The day before, the carpet had no smell, and if it did he would've asked to change rooms, because noises, images, tastes, all distracted and could even derail his entire day, but nothing could send him spiraling the way a smell often did. The bathroom door was open when he left, but only enough to see the toilet paper roll. He did that because when the housekeeping came they would always fold it with the end pointed like an arrow. He could see that the toilet paper dangled the way he had left it.

Husky

He never left his computer open. Not once. It wasn't just a privacy issue. It was so that if someone had knocked it over, the damage was minimized with a closed screen, and he always pointed the remote to the TV away from the door. That was something his mother had done. "I don't trust them," she always said. "They shoot rays at you." So he never left it pointing at the door. Just in case.

Golden Doodle

The lamp had been a sconce, and the phone was white, not black. No one had been in the room but him, and he had not left it in such disarray.

"We're still in the house."

"Aye, boy," the voice came from the figurine. "You tink I just let you go?"

Eddie dropped his keys and backpack.

"Just because you take care of my soldier?" The thick Cajun accent turned "soldier" into "sul-jah." The figurine glowed. "You nevah lef me. Dis time you ain' gon git away."

"Stop it!" Eddie pressed his hands against his ears.

"Wake up boy," the voice said. "I git tired'a waitin'."

He turned to leave the room and was met with a mob of rednecks storming his hotel room. They grabbed him and pinned him to the bed. One in the back launched a torch into the room, sending everything into flames.

"Burn them all! Burn them all!"

The crowd parted, giving a large skinhead room. He raised a pitchfork over his head and brought its spikes down on Eddie's face.

Eddie bolted upright panting. He lay in front of the fire in the Nelson House. The hurricane was like an avalanche on the ceiling. He backed against a wall and folded himself into a ball.

17

Rose Colline Chevy

Jess got back in the car and waited for Eddie to open the door before she pulled out of her parking spot. Eddie wasn't someone who would leave his things somewhere, but she did it anyway. When Eddie was inside, she pulled away.

"Man, Crazy Eddie," Duke said. "I don't think I've seen him since graduation."

"We haven't either," Carlos said. "He went to college, and we didn't go anywhere."

"I love that guy," Duke said with a smile brandished across his face. "Don't tell him I said that though. I'd never tell him to his face."

"Why wouldn't you tell him that?" Jess asked. She sounded sad.

"Well, I mean, look how awkward he gets when just talks. Me-and-him ain't like y'all-and-him. He's quiet, and I don't know how to get him to open up like he does with y'all."

"Have you even tried being quiet with him?" Jess said.

"Or just at all," Carlos joked.

"I mean it," Jess said. "He used to sit at the lunch table, and I would just sit with him. That's all it takes. He doesn't bond your way. That'll never work. He doesn't get humor."

Duke only heard Jess say that he was funny.

"You got to do it his way."

"I'm sure that's true," Duke said. Out the window, a black shape appeared in the trees. "Whoa, did y'all see that?"

"See what?" Carlos asked.

"I think it was that thing."

"We're going like sixty," Carlos said. "I don't think it was that thing."

"We were stopped for like ten minutes," Duke said. "Plus, cheetahs can run like ninety-five miles per hour or something."

"I don't think it was a cheetah," Jess said. She snatched glances out the driver's side window, looking for any signs of the thing that Duke had seen. She thought of the way it had the deer by the neck and shuddered. "Too big."

"Maybe," Duke said. He could see the turn that led to Rose Colline Chevy. "Why don't you just drop me off at work, I'll take the company car, and y'all won't have to drive all the way out to the house."

"You're not going to go looking for that thing, are you?" Jess accused.

"Don't do that, Duke."

"Nah, I'm just saying," Duke said, holding his hands up as if to show that no tricks were being played. Really, he was using an old sales trick. Take what they want and make them want it even more. Make it their idea. Then act like you're doing them a favor by letting them have it. "That was a rough night. You already said you wanted to see your daughter. Why don't you just drop me off and go get little Dommy. It's another fifteen miles to my place. That's way out of your way. Just head on home."

Jess and Carlos made eye contact. "You sure?" Carlos asked.

"Come on, man," Duke said. Make a joke and close this thing. "I see how you are with that kid. You can't wait to bounce her on your weird little leg. It's no big deal. I'll take the company car the rest of the way."

Jess made the silent decision to turn.

"Oh, that's right," Carlos said. "We've got the future owner of Rose Colline Chevy in our midst, hon."

"That's right," Duke said proudly. "Soon as the old man retires, he's leaving it to me."

"You didn't tell me that, hon," Jess said. She was a little too enthusiastic, and Duke knew it was partially genuine and partially because he had just "done them a favor."

"Very excited," Duke said.

"Ton of money?" Carlos asked. Jess tapped him playfully on the arm. "I don't need to know anything specific."

"More than I get now that's for sure," Duke said. He pointed to the front door. "Just right here. I have a key in my office."

The car slowed to a stop and Duke got out. Carlos met him at the back of the Outback.

"Let me know when you want to upgrade this thing."

"We'll see," Carlos said, laughing. "Thanks for coming. I

don't think we could've done without you getting shot in the face three times."

"Hey," Duke said. He was being serious for once. It took Carlos by surprise. "Look, can I tell you something? Just between us?"

"Yeah, man."

"If you don't cut off that fuckin' mustache, I'll do it for you. Is she doing this to you?"

"Thanks, Duke,"

"Seriously, I'll come in your sleep. Take the whole lip."

Duke hugged Carlos's neck and waved them off.

He locked the glass door behind him. The alarm wasn't sounding, and he made a mental note to write up whoever closed yesterday afternoon. Duke crossed the showroom to his office. He turned on the light and dug through his desk. It was darker than he remembered, and were the handles on the drawers this shiny? He ignored it.

Duke found the key to the company truck and closed his desk drawer. He paused, reopened the drawer and grabbed the pistol and holster from under a folder. He stood from the desk, wondering who had cleaned it. Nothing was out of order. In fact, none of his things, not even the Terry Bradshaw bobblehead, were on his desk. He turned to the bookshelf behind him where he kept a plant and a few awards—no books—and there was the Terry Bradshaw bobblehead. Its head bobbled slightly as if at the thought of it being missing, someone had tried to sneak it in behind him.

Just the AC. I must have moved it and forgot.

He replaced the bobblehead in its spot between his monitor and the phone. He walked to the door, looking to see if he had moved anything else and forgot to move it back. Something was off but he couldn't figure it out.

You're here at eight in the morning, he thought. *No one will be in for another forty-five minutes. Probably just too quiet, and it's definitely too early. Stop freaking yourself out.*

Duke set the alarm on his way out, and it warbled as if the speaker was underwater.

He made a note to get someone to look at that.

Duke was focused, and when he became focused on something, he became obsessed with it. The company truck was parked by the loading bay behind the building. He got in it and pulled out of the lot, noticing how clean it was.

I don't care if they cleaned it, that's no excuse for forgetting the alarm.

He pulled back on the road, keeping one eye pinned to the woods. He saw nothing. Nothing black, nothing moving, not so much as a bird flying across the windshield. He passed Eddie's hotel. The parking lot was empty, and he wondered where everyone, including Eddie, had gone. It was almost as if the hotel had gone out of business in the last ten minutes.

Duke slowed the truck and pulled over into the ditch when he saw the deer in the road. He got out and examined it. The hole in its neck was gruesomely bloody. Bugs had already infiltrated the carcass and the smell made Duke gag. He backed away before the need to vomit stormed up his esophagus and into the road. He looked for a clearing or an opening in the trees. A thing that big had to have made some kind of impact on the brush as it ran off into the woods. All he could find was some recently kicked up grass at the tree line.

There was a briar patch there that the thing could've easily stepped over. Duke noticed a small drop of blood, still fresh, on a thorn.

It's go time. I don't know what it is, but I want it on my wall.

Duke had never hunted anything with a handgun, but he had died three times the night before. If he could make it through that, what could stop him?

He crossed into the woods. Birds sang their songs, but he didn't see any. He wasn't necessarily looking for them either. Leaves crunched under foot, and he wondered why it wasn't wetter in the woods if a hurricane had just blown through. It was a little odd that there were no fallen trees that he could see. Even a category 1 knocked over the flimsy ones. Katrina was a five in the Gulf, and it didn't even wet the ground?

Then Duke saw something dart away from him. The shape weaved through the trees with the speed and grace of a deer. Duke sprang into action, following the shape. He saw it moving through the trees, ducking back and forth between bushes and thick tree trunks. He listened for the crunch of his footfalls.

A chitter, almost a laugh, sounded through the air. Duke sped up. He trained the pistol ahead of him, searching for any movement. Something ran across his vision a few dozen feet away, and on instinct he fired the gun. Bark shot out of a trunk, raining on the ground. The thing chittered again. He saw it and fired, but it was quick and ducked into a hole in the ground.

Fuckin' thing is laughing at me.

Duke followed the gun to the hole in the ground. Inside the hole was a set of perfectly carved steps. Duke kicked a stick down the hole and waited for something to happen. The woods fell silent. Duke held his breath. A few moments passed and as Duke exhaled, the thing chittered. This time it actually was laughing at him.

"This is bullshit," Duke said. He cocked the gun, only now remembering that it was a revolver. "Get over here you little asshole."

Duke descended the stairs.

Darkness surrounded him. He used the flashlight keychain to light up a few feet of space ahead of him. He turned back, looking up the stairs. The few steps he thought he had taken turned out to be a few flights of stairs. The hole he had entered the stairway from was dozens of feet away.

"That's weird. Must've zoned out."

"Is that what happened, Duke?"

"Who the fuck is that?" Duke demanded. He pointed the gun into the darkness.

"It's me, Kevin."

"Kevin is gone, man," Duke said, sounding stupid even to himself.

"I'm right here, Duke."

A hand grabbed Duke on the shoulder. He spun around, dropping the keys down the stairs, and fired the gun into the black. In the flash of the bullet shot, he saw nothing but an empty stairwell. Chips of stone pelted his face. He felt on the stairs for the keys. He felt nothing.

"Not that way," Kevin's voice called. "I'm over here."

Above him the way out was gone. Duke turned back to

the voice and descended the stairs after it, feeling with his foot for the keys. He took a step and swept back and forth listening for a jingle. Took a step, sweep. Step, sweep. Step…

His foot connected with something. A leg.

"See," Kevin said. "Here I am."

Duke heard the jingle of the keys. He felt the air move as Kevin raised them to his face.

"I missed you, buddy," Kevin said.

The light shown on his face. Kevin's eyes were white and glossed over with death. Black veins stood out in this face. He smiled an inhuman, wide smile with teeth that were dirty and sharp like rusty daggers. He wore the shirt with the cut-off sleeves, and the golden earring glinted. The hand holding the keychain was consumed with decay, and the smell of rot and death infiltrated Duke's senses. Duke shrieked and fired the gun. The light went out. The chitter came to him. It attacked in the dark.

Duke fired the gun. Over and over in defense.

He heard the screams of Eddie, Jess, and Churro.

"Put down the goddamn gun, Duke." Churro shouted.

Lightning boomed, and Duke froze. He looked at the gun he was holding in the light from the fireplace. It was solid white ivory and warm from the shots he had fired. He looked at them.

"I—"

Their faces were horrified.

"I'm sorry." It came as a whisper, and he cleared his throat. "I'm sorry."

18

Come Smoke a Bowl with Me

Carlos got back in the car, and when Duke entered the dealership, Jess backed the car out of the lot. She backtracked past the hotel to Carlos's mother's trailer. He looked to Jess, and they made the same quiet eye contact they did on their first date.

They passed the dead deer in the road, and Carlos heard a swell of cicada buzzes so loud it vibrated against the car. He shook his nerves away. Before he could spend too much thought on the noise, Jess spoke up.

"Tell me something, and be honest."

"Anything," Carlos said. "Shoot."

"Did we ever cuss as much as Duke?"

They laughed. It was the emotional drain neither of them realized they needed.

"Probably, yeah," Carlos said. "I think he just never grew out of it."

"It's just 'fuck, fuck, fuck' with him," Jess laughed. "Although after two years, I feel good. Why did I ever stop?"

"Because you're a good mom."

Jess smiled. "Shut up. I'm gonna cry." She laughed, but just under the surface, tears were preparing to overflow. She changed the subject. "How'd it feel answering to Churro, again?"

Carlos breathed a chuckle. "I guess you can't leave everything back in your childhood."

"Maybe we can bring it back," Jess grinned at him. For a flash, it seemed too wide. Carlos didn't react, but it was almost like a caricature of his wife's grin. Her lips pulled all the way across her face beyond her cheeks to the side of her head beneath her cherry red hair. Her green eyes were too big. It was like looking at a weird dreamed up memory of his wife. He blinked and it was normal again.

Fuck, I need sleep. And that does feel good. Jess's eyes are blue.

"I tell you what," Carlos said. "You can call me Churro, but I want to rename Dominique Chorizo Chipotle Rosita Flores."

"Oh, my God," Jess said. Her laughter almost caused her to swerve off the road.

"It's that or no deal," Carlos said. "Actually no, I will settle for making her middle name 'con Pollo' if I have to." They laughed together.

"I'll be honest with you," Carlos said. "I didn't expect it to be such a nice day after a hurricane. It's hardly even wet outside. I thought surely I'd be up to my ass in phone calls."

Jess turned onto the trailer park's road, and her phone buzzed in the cup holder. She answered it, her tone turned sour. She stopped the car at Wayway's trailer. She got off the phone. "Shit," she said. "I'm sorry. I have to go put out a fire at the daycare."

"A literal one?" Carlos said.

"Yeah," Jess said, coldly.

"You don't want to see your daughter first," Carlos asked.

"I can't," Jess said. "Kiss her for me."

"Okay, weirdo." Carlos kissed her and left the car.

He knocked on the door of the trailer. When he turned around Jess was already gone. He hadn't even heard her back away. Dominique made two-year-old noises on the other side of the door.

His mother opened the door, holding her by thc foot.

"Shit, mom. What the hell?"

"Oh, it's nothing," she told him. "We've been playing this all night. Nobody got hurt."

"You're going to dislocate her leg." Carlos scooped Dominique in his arms. Her green eyes shined with happiness.

Her eyes look just like her mother's. How did I never notice that?

"Come on in. Come on in," Isabella said, waved him inside. "Knock those boots off. I don't want you to go traipsing mud all through the house."

Jess's eyes are blue.

Carlos looked at his daughter again. Her caramel eyes looked back at him in wonder. "I need a nap," he said.

"Come in here and talk to me first, dear," Isabella said. "Come smoke a bowl with me."

"Mom, I can't do that anymore."

"Don't bullshit me. I know what you do. That little girl will be fine for two minutes."

He sat Dominique on the couch. "I'm not doing that. I have a kid."

"I had you," she said.

"Yeah," Carlos said, looking around the dingy trailer. "Yeah, I guess that's true."

"Sit," she said. A joint jutted from her mouth like a toothpick. She struck her lighter.

Something wouldn't let Carlos follow his instinct to scoop Dominique up and storm out. Something told him this was normal, that she smoked weed in the house when he was still Churro, and that turned out alright.

"Fine," he said. He pulled one of the patio chairs out from under the card table. He noticed that she was wearing a turtleneck in August. "You don't smoke around Dom, do you?"

"Can I tell you something that's always bothered me?"

"Okay," Carlos said. He noticed her typically broken English was suddenly much better. The table was covered with burn marks. "You feeling alright mom?"

Isabella inhaled. She held the smoke in her lungs. "Yeah," she blew the smoke in Carlos's face. "Why wouldn't I be?"

"Well, you never smoke inside, you're wearing a sweater, and you're bleeding behind your ears." Carlos reached up to her face. She sucked in another lungful of smoke. She didn't smell like pot, only fire. He touched the blood dripping down the side of her face. She exhaled the smoke, but it didn't leave her mouth. It billowed from her neck. The smoke burned his eyes and filled the room. He couldn't see where Dominique was anymore.

"Let me tell you what's always bothered me." Isabella took another drag on the joint. "That first night you brought that white girl into this house, I was so furious with you."

Her fist slammed down on the table. Carlos tried to stand up, but something had bound him to the patio furniture.

"Just sit there and listen."

"If you had a problem with her, you had ten years to say something about it before now."

Why is that what you're worried about? Get Dom, and get the fuck out of here.

"That's why your father killed himself, you know," Isabella said.

Carlos couldn't even see her now. Smoke was everywhere. His eyes burned. "Dad died from a cocaine overdose."

"Why do you think he was doing drugs in the first place? He was ashamed of you."

The voice morphed into something gruff, masculine. He heard something clamping together.

"No, he wasn't. He gave a speech. At the wedding." Carlos's head swam. The smoke was getting him high. He pulled on his wrists, but whatever held him was thick. He tried to stand but his legs were bound to the chair.

Isabella slammed her fist on the table again.

"You fucked the first thing that would touch your little

pecker and gave up. Now I have to babysit a little mutt. But I don't want it! I don't want this stupid baby. So let me fix it for the both of us!"

Dom's giggle resounded through the smoke, and the room fell completely silent. A thick, veiny hand swung the toddler by the leg. Carlos screamed, falling back onto the floor. The aluminum chair shattered into flotsam. The hand swung again, striking Carlos across his face. His daughter giggled.

Through the smoke, the child flew at him. The mouth stretched across its face like a demonic puppet with stakes for teeth. It latched onto Carlos's neck.

"Stop squirming, Churro!"

Footsteps pounded toward him. His mother charged him, her face black with decay. Her skin sagged off her skull. He braced himself with his hands, and they plunged into her neck. He went to the ground with her clamping her jagged, black teeth in his face. Slobber dripped in his face. The blood from her neck soaked his clothes.

Her teeth clamped again. The sound grew louder and louder until gunshots exploded in his mind.

clamp

clam

bam

BAM!

He winced away from the thing his mother had become. He felt the drool on his face.

When he opened his eyes he was back in the Nelson House. His mother was gone, but the sound of clamp continued.

He scrambled to his feet. Jess screamed. Duke was firing the ivory revolver into the ceiling. Eddie trembled in the corner of the room.

"Duke!" he screamed.

Duke snapped awake.

"Put down the goddamn gun, Duke!"

"I—," Duke stammered. "I'm sorry."

19

Jess

Jess turned onto the trailer park's road, and Carlos's phone buzzed in the cup holder. He answered it, his tone turned sour. She stopped the car at Wayway's trailer. Carlos got off the phone. "Shit," he said. "I'm sorry. I have to go put out a fire at the downtown."

She snorted a laugh, "A literal one?"

"I think."

"Well, come say hey to the baby real quick and you can go."

"I don't think I have time."

"Carlos, it's your child," Jess said. "You could've died, and we don't even know if this is over. It'll take two seconds to kiss your child and you can take the car. I want to thank your mother for watching her, but you don't have to stay for all that."

Carlos's eyes widened as he visibly struggled to find an argument. "Okay, yeah."

Jess's brow furrowed. She got out of the car eyeballing

him. "Why are you being weird about it? I never have to make you stay."

"It's a fire."

"You're not a firefighter." Jess tossed him the keys to the car.

"Yeah, I probably won't be able to help much. You're right."

"Yeah," she agreed. She climbed the porch steps and knocked on the door. "I would think you'd want to see her as bad as I do."

Jess turned back to him, but the car was gone. She hadn't even heard it crank.

Something's wrong. This isn't right.

But she couldn't grasp what wasn't right. Like something else oversaw reality. It felt like a dream, one where something strange happened, but before it could be addressed, something even weirder happened to make you forget it.

She knocked on the door again, looking for the car—thinking it couldn't have gone that far—but her knuckles met nothing but air. The trailer door was open and the hazy, washed out view forced her inside.

Oh, God. The house is burning, and my baby is in here all alone.

"Isabella!" Jess called. She stormed into the trailer.

In the floor of the living room, there was an impressively erected couch cushion fort. A bedsheet draped over the outside like the cover of a circus tent. Two little feet jutted out from under the sheet wearing socks with little mouse faces sewn on the outside. Jess lifted the sheet.

Dominique lay with her thumb plugged in her mouth. The tension in Jess melted away. She reached under the cushions and pulled the thumb out of her daughter's mouth. Dominique wriggled in protest but left her hand on the pillow.

Jess crawled under the sheet and laid down next to her daughter. She put her nose against her head and smelled deeply. This is real. She would never forget that smell, and nothing could ever imitate it—not even another baby. That specific smell was printed on Jess's mind and was kept in a very special place with Carlos's birthday, her memories of Kevin, and unfortunately everything that happened in the Nelson House. Somehow a recipe for buffalo chicken wraps managed to hide away in that section of her mind. She shook away the nonsense in favor of enjoying this moment with Dom.

Then she remembered the haze that had blurred her view. The way it smelled faintly like fire when she first saw through the open door. She sat up from the fort and scanned the room. Things were just off enough for her to simultaneously notice and forgive. Sure, she could've moved these things, the entertainment shelf for instance. Just yesterday it had been all the way against the divider between the living room and kitchen. Not it was far enough away from that wall to be overlapping the window. It was more centered in the room now. But maybe Isabella did it for Dom's sake. Maybe they had just decided to move the pictures on the walls to center those two. Perhaps that was the way Dominique ruled from her pillow fort.

Jess giggled internally at the idea of her little tyke ruling with an iron fist, having ice cream *before* chicken nuggets every night at dinner.

Her reverie was broken by the sound of something heavy dropping on the floor.

Jess's attention snapped to that side of the trailer. She could see a body, and through the haze she could tell it was Isabella.

"Wayway," she called, apprehension swelling like a toothache.

The sensation of a nose bleed hit her. She touched her nostril, and her finger came away dry. The sensation went away, but the smell didn't.

"Wayway, you okay?" Jess got to her feet.

Blood spread in an amoeba shape around Isabella. Jess fell to her knees, uttering a weak cry. She instinctively covered her mouth to remain as quiet as possible so she wouldn't wake Dom.

Do not wake the baby. Whatever you do, don't wake Dom. This is exactly the kind of thing that will stick with her. Do you want this to be her earliest memory? Compose yourself.

She quietly dragged herself to the body. The smell of blood was overwhelming. She saw the face, and a brand-new wave of dread hit her as she confirmed that this was Isabella. That feeling didn't stop at realization. It grew as the picture became focused. Isabella's face had been mutilated. Her skin had been removed in patches all the way down her body. The patches were precise as if cut out with an incredibly sharp blade.

A crash.

It came from deeper in the trailer. Jess looked down the hallway and noticed something on the wall. It was oozing. She stood and approached the square thing. It was skin, stuck to the wall with nothing but the viscosity of Isabella's blood. She tried to stop herself from touching it, but her arm wouldn't react to her brain's command. She touched the rubbery skin. The skin fell off the wall, and her empty stomach wretched.

Grab Dominique and get out. Get her and go.

Jess rounded back to the living room. What she saw was a clearing. Stone. And in the stone, two circles had been carved out, one inside the other, and in the center, standing like a dart on a bullseye, there stood a wooden statue of a man with dreadlocks and a top hat. His eyes were sunken, and his cheekbones were sharp as if the man were emaciated. The statue wore a suit with holes in it, and there was something like tissue stuffed in his nose. He held a staff in one hand and a bottle of rum in the other.

Jess stood looking into the clearing, perplexed.

This isn't real.

"I took her you know."

Jess spun around.

Standing behind her in a muddy hospital jumpsuit, Jamie held a boxcutter dripping with blood. "I came here when he let me out. I killed the old lady and I took her. Your daughter."

"What? I just saw her."

"You already know this isn't real," Jamie scoffed.

"You're sitting in the Nelson House trying to wake up from all this right now."

"Where'd you take her?" Jess said. Her voice dropped. Her head lowered, ready to strike out. Ready to beat the box cutter out of Jamie's hand, and cut squares of flesh out of her face.

"Oh, I'm bringing her to you." Jamie dropped the box cutter in the sand. She smiled with bloody teeth. "God is going to use the kid and bring me to Heaven. Your brother's coming too. He waited all these years until we were ready. God provides."

"What the fuck are you talking about?"

"And I punish."

Jamie charged forward, her eye glazing over with white. Black like venom filled the veins in her neck and face. Her teeth clamped together like a bear trap. She grabbed Jess and bit down hard on her shoulder.

The pain was white hot. None of this was real. Jamie wasn't real. The clearing wasn't real. But the pain in her shoulder as Jamie ripped and tore at the muscle, was real. It electrified.

Jess snapped awake to the dusty, warm room of the Nelson House. She heaved breath, trying to stabilize her fury and heart.

Lightning crashed, and she saw Eddie balled in the corner. She went to him. "Eddie, you okay?" He nodded, whimpering quietly. She wrapped an arm around him. Carlos groaned and turned over on the floor. Tears stood in her eyes. She blinked them away. "Yeah, me too."

"I thought it was over."

"I did too," Jess said. Thunder shook the walls.

Duke groaned and raised something toward the ceiling. She shouted in defiance of everything living, and Duke fired the ivory revolver.

Carlos jerked awake. "Duke!"

Duke fired the revolver into the ceiling again. And again.

"Duke!"

Duke sat up, fully awake.

"Put down the goddamn gun, Duke!" Carlos said.

"I—," Duke stammered. He looked at Jess and Eddie who was cowering. Tears stood in his eyes, and in thaat moment, Jess felt with Duke for the first time in their adult lives. Nothing summed how she felt—how they all felt—like the look on his face right then. "I'm sorry." He cleared his throat. "I'm sorry."

20

Stroller Through the Woods

Jamie left the trailer, having put Dominique in a stroller. She walked out the back door carrying the stroller and then put it down in the fallen leaves. Rain fell on them. Using only the moonlight and the brief flashes the weather gave her, she reentered the woods with Dominique in her possession.

Dominique pouted as the rain fell on her mouse socks.

"Don't start yet," Jamie said. "It's going to get a lot worse before it stops."

"Pops," Dominique replied. She giggled and shook her little bottom. Her chubby hands clapped with each repeat of the word. "Pops. Pops. Pops, pops, pops."

"That's right. Pop, pop, pop," Jamie encouraged. The green glow of her eyes faded to darkness. "Punish. Punish. Punish."

She followed the path laid by the neighborhood dogs. From here she would have to make a considerable trek with a baby stroller through the woods back to the Nelson House.

The path began to narrow. Bushes and low hanging branches reached out toward the stroller. Jamie frowned at their attempts to reach the baby—to make the baby impure for her god. An unseen vine with thorns blocked the path, and Jamie pushed the stroller right into it. Dominique cried loudly.

"No, no, no, no, no," Jamie said. She ran around the stroller. She saw the vine and yanked it out of the ground. Her hands bleeding now, she showed Dominique the harmlessness of the vine. She dropped it on the ground and stomped, sending fresh pain up her leg. Dominique took no notice and cried harder. "No, please. No."

Jamie paced back and forth, she tripped over a root and went sprawling in mud. Dominique blatted and blew raspberries. The crying had stopped. Jamie got up and moved to the stroller. "Yes?" she balled up her fist, and bonked her own head, crossing her eyes in make-believe pain.

Dominique giggled. It was a happy noise that meant Jamie's salvation.

Jamie stood and bonked her head again, but this time she fell sprawling out on the ground.

Dominique kicked and clapped with laughter. "Funny."

Jamie got to her feet, beaming.

"Are you taking me to my mommy?"

"No," Jamie said, slowly shaking her head.

"Are you taking me home?"

"Yes," Jamie nodded, excitedly.

"Okay," Dominique said. "Mommy. See mommy."

Jamie took her place behind the stroller. She wasn't certain where to go then. The path was too narrow for the stroller.

"Wet!" Dominique pouted.

Jamie looked for a spot to get out of the rain. She had to think. She had to get back to the Nelson House before her god changed his mind about her. And he had already done so much. It was time to pay him back. She looked to the tree tops for a patch of growth that wouldn't allow much rain to fall on them. She found one and pushed the stroller beneath it.

"That better," Dominique cheered.

"Yes," Jamie agreed. Something took over her then. Shared her body with her.

Are you hungry?

Jamie lit up. Her heart races as if from the touch of a high school crush.

If you are hungry, I will provide.

"Yes," she whispered.

They will try to stop you.

Jamie's brow furrowed. "No," she growled.

No. You won't let them. Be prepared to fight for me. Are you still my champion?

"Yes," she whispered.

Then come. Come and I will provide.

Jamie felt the presence leave. She gripped the stroller's handlebar, suddenly overwhelmed with anger. How could they do this? How could they leave her in that room for so long, and now that she's free of it, how could they stop her from doing as her god bids?

How dare they.

"Hungry," Dominique said. Her hands rubbed at her eyes. She lay still and fell back to sleep.

I will provide.

Jamie looked to the treetops. Lightning flashed, and she saw a path overhead where the brush would protect them from the rain. She followed it, not looking down at the ground, but up to the trees, and to her god. Quicker now, she moved through the woods to the Nelson House.

"Punish. Punish. Punish."

21

He's a Trickster

"We were out," Duke said, mesmerized by his position in the universe. "I had the gun, I shot the Sofi octopus."

"We saw you," Carlos said.

"And we left," Duke finished. "Why are we still here?"

"We never left, Duke," Jess said.

"Obviously," he answered. "Well, what the fuck? We did our part."

"There's something else," Eddie said. "It's stronger."

"What is it, Eddie?" Jess said. They watched him turning the Rubik's Cube nervously in the light of the fire.

"I saw something. I heard it actually. I was in my hotel room. It came from a statue my producer gave me. It was a pewter statue of the voodoo figures Baron Samedi and Papa Legba. Some stupid knickknack I was probably supposed to put on my desk, but I hate it, so I use it to center myself." Eddie looked at them. "Sorry. That's not the point. They're kind of like St. Peter and the Angel of Death in Catholicism. The part of the statue that spoke to me was the Baron Samedi figure. He wears a top hat and drinks rum from the bottle. He spoke to me."

"You talking to statues now, Crazy Eddie?"

"No, I saw something like that too," Jess interjected. "It had to be. He didn't speak to me though."

"Did we all see something?" Duke asked, mostly the question was for himself.

"I saw a thing," Carlos said, concentrating.

"Good start," Duke said.

"No, it was like a panther or something."

"Me too," Duke said. "I followed it into a hole in the woods. There were stairs that led down to God knows where, and I saw Kevin. As much as anything could be Kevin at this point."

"I saw a clearing," Jess said. "It was dark. The ground was cold and there were circles carved into the ground. And in the middle was a wooden statue like you said, Eddie."

"That has to be it," Carlos said. "That has to be what we're dealing with. What else do you know, Eddie?"

"He's from the crossroads between our world and the land of the dead. He dresses in funeral clothes so that he can go undetected in either world. He is the master of the dead and uses them to do his bidding. He's a trickster. Debaucherous. He makes deals with you for your soul, and if you outsmart him, he cheats to get it anyway."

"Right," Duke said. "So that's what we're dealing with then. A weird fuckin' deal-making swindler. This shouldn't be too difficult."

"How do we even begin to deal with this?" Jess said.

"I think he told us," Eddie said. "He showed us. Each one of us saw something different. I don't think they were meant to be separate. I think we have to put them all together."

"Okay," Carlos said. "Eddie, you were in your hotel room, what else?"

"Some rednecks came in and set the room on fire."

"I saw the stairway," Duke said. "It was dark, and it led down to somewhere."

"Probably the clearing I saw. And the statue was wooden."

"There we go" Carlos said. "We've got to find the stairs to the clearing and set the thing on fire."

"Sweet," Duke said. He pointed the revolver at the stairs in the foyer. He noticed that the gun was starting to rust. "Only, the only stairs we have go up, not down."

"We'll just have to find some more," Carlos said.

"Where?" Duke asked. "There are like four rooms in the whole house."

"Maybe there's something under the floor," Jess said.

"Or what if we just went down the stairs?" Duke asked. This was the one time he was being serious. "Wait for him to do his weird…mindfuck thing."

"That's only stupid when you first hear it," Jess said after a moment's thought. "You try that, we'll start digging up the boards."

"We should probably leave the door open," Carlos said. "That weird thing Duke said makes since. If we keep it open it'll anchor us to the real world."

"Yeah, another thing," Duke began. "Something's wrong with the gun. It's rusting."

"Must be because you're holding it," Carlos said. "Not him. If you just feel better with a gun, there's one in the car you can go get."

"I think we should try not to separate this time," Eddie said. "At least we'll be together."

"Well, you will have to go down without me," Jess said. They stared at her, bewildered. "I saw something else. Jamie. She's out."

"What?" Carlos asked, not expecting an answer.

"She took Dom," Jess continued. "She's coming here. Leave the door open. I want to see her coming."

22

Weather Pattern

They had searched for what felt like an hour, going over every inch of the house looking for secret entrances, when they finally resorted to digging through the floor looking for holes. There was nothing in the kitchen. None of the rooms had anything but dust and a single dead snake. One of the rooms was growing mold on the floor as if rain water had dripped there over the years. They decided to dig through the floor. Carlos had brandished a hammer and crowbar from his backpack. "After the first one comes up the others will be easy to pry up."

"Be careful," Jess said, standing between the living room and the foyer. Her arms were nervously folded over one another. She turned away and watched Duke walk up and down the stairs, waiting for something to happen. "Anything happening over there, Duke?"

"My glutes are on fire," Duke said between gasps of air.

"Make your mom proud."

"Here we go," Carlos said. He wedged the end of the crowbar between two floorboards and drove the hammer down on it.

Lightning flickered, and something outside caught Eddie's eye. Thunder sent a wave of vibration through the house. They felt it like energy under their feet. Eddie opened the back door. He looked through the clearing between the trees overhead. A pattern had formed in the clouds. Jess crossed the living room and put a hand on his shoulder, more to keep him in sight than because she was worried that he'd leave.

"What's going on, Eddie?" Jess tried to see what he was seeing, but this was something only Eddie's mind would be able to process.

"It's the layout of the house," Eddie said. He sounded like he was dreaming. "It's in the clouds." Lightning flashed over him, simultaneously pointing to a very specific spot in the layout and burning it into his vision. He blinked and the remains of the vision flashed in front of his eyes.

"Eddie, are you okay?" Jess said, in a panic. She pulled him back in and shut the door.

"I've got it," Eddie said. He walked to the fireplace and found a single brick that had been split into two pieces. One of the pieces jutted out just enough to make the surface uneven. He pressed it back into formation and the burning wood in the fireplace dropped. They could still see its orange and red aura, but it dwindled as the pieces rolled down the steps underneath.

"Holy shit," Carlos said. "Eddie, you are cooler than I know."

"Duke," Jess called. "Eddie found it."

"Duke," Carlos said loudly.

His footsteps on the rickety stairs had fallen silent.

23

Punish. Punish. Punish.

When the Nelson House finally came into the view, elation brightened Jamie's face. She hopped with excitement. Dominique rested quietly under the rubber cover of the stroller. The front door was wide open, and she saw a face she recognized moving through the lantern light. It was Duke. He was with her the first time she ever came to the Nelson House, him, and Eddie, and Churro, and Jess, and…

Kevin was her boyfriend. They had watched the house burn down, and if her god could bring the house back, he could bring him back. She allowed herself a moment of excitement. Then the voice of her god spoke up in her mind.

They will try to stop you.

She gripped the handle of the stroller. Her muscles stood out like ropes.

"Punish. Punish. Punish."

Jamie pushed the stroller to the porch. She picked it up and hid Dominique in the corner out of sight. She drew the box cutter from her pocket and darted across the doorway.

The footsteps inside clomped up the stairs, then down.

She tapped on the doorframe. The footsteps stopped. She tapped again, put a rhythm to it this time.

"Y'all hear that?"

The footsteps came to the door.

Be my champion.

Duke breeched the doorway. He surveyed the porch and noticed the stroller nearly in the rain. He rushed over.

Jamie sprinted across the porch on the balls of her feet. Duke spun around, and Jamie used the box cutter. It severed his vocal chords, and he couldn't scream for help.

She pulled him by the hair to meet her eyes. "You left me. To die."

The disbelief on Duke's face briefly touched the real Jamie's heart.

Be my champion.

The boxcutter rammed through the bottom of Duke's mouth, and the life left his eyes.

"Punish. Punish. Punish."

Jamie dropped his body off the porch into the wet leaves. Something fell off the body. It was white and looked old and rusty. Jamie stepped off the porch. She nudged it with her toe.

Take it. Become my champion.

Jamie took the revolver. She held it, felt its weight. That weight meant purpose, something she never truly had. Her finger squeezed the trigger and fired a round into the sky. Rain dripped into the barrel. A rush pulsed through her body in waves of pleasure. She spun and aimed at the house.

24

Chitter

"He's probably just upstairs screwing around." Carlos gathered his tools and picked up a lantern. "This is only going to leave you with one. You going to be okay up here?"

"That thing wants my baby," Jess said. "She'll be bringing her through that door, and I won't let her get beyond."

"You're such a badass." Carlos kissed her. "Send Duke this way if you find him."

Eddie crawled into the fireplace first. The soot stained his fingers and face.

Carlos handed him a lantern. "What do you see, Ed?"

"Stone walls. Dust. Spiderwebs. Stairs. Rocks."

"That's good, bud." Carlos said. He descended into the fireplace and said to Jess, "Scream if you need us, I guess."

"I can't see the end," Eddie said.

"Let's try this," Carlos said. He bent down and picked up an old piece of wood. He whipped it over Eddie's head, and they listened to it bounce down the steps. It eventually stopped on a step somewhere below. "Well, I guess we better get going."

They descended the steps for longer than either of them could count. They heard a chitter.

Eddie stopped. Carlos bumped into him. "It's not real, bud."

"How do you know?"

"You died today," Carlos said plainly. "Does that make a lot of sense?"

"No."

"Then it's not real. If you can't justify it, it must not be real."

Eddie continued.

"I'm real, Eddie." It chittered and giggled. It was Kevin. "Don't you remember me?"

"Just keep going, Eddie."

Eddie pressed forward.

"Yes!" Kevin shrieked. "Keep going!" He charged them and grabbed them with impossibly strong hands. He smelled like decay. His rotten smile was missing more teeth than it had. He dragged them by the neck down the stairs. Their bodies pounded on the steps. Kevin cackled. Eddie swung the lantern, striking Kevin in the chest. The lantern shattered, lighting Kevin ablaze. He roared in pain. The stone walls cracked and crumbled around them.

Carlos felt his body jerk as Kevin launched them down the stairs. He and Eddie bounced off the stone floor. Carlos's backpack opened on impact, sending tools flying across the chamber. He cradled the lantern, protecting it with his body, and when he landed, his ribs cracked. He couldn't lift himself off the floor.

Eddie stood up, looking around the room. In the lantern light, he could make out the circles carved out of the floor. Standing in the center was a wooden totem carved to match the pewter figure of Baron Samedi that waited, crooked, on the dresser in his hotel.

"Welcome back," a shape appeared from the darkness.

"Carlos," Eddie said, standing over him. "Get up. I can't do this by myself."

"What a stupid mustache."

25

Fire

Jess waited at the fireplace until she could no longer hear Eddie's and Carlos's voices. She paced through the lower level of the house, keeping her eye on the door. She checked the kitchen through the swinging door. Nothing but dust and mold.

"Duke!" Jess called up the stairs. There was no answer, but the revolver blasted outside. "Duke, get back in here. You're going to shoot yourself with that thing."

She stopped, glaring out the door. Something rolled across the porch. Dominique's stroller came into view. She instinctively went to her daughter, forgetting what she was waiting for, when Jamie pointed the gun at her and fired. The bullet whizzed by her head. Dominique woke up.

"Mommy!"

"Dom, baby, I need you to be quiet, okay?" She wasn't looking at her daughter, just the mad woman pointing a two -hundred-year-old gun at her.

"Punish. Punish. Punish."

"Jamie," Jess said, focusing on being calm, because the alternative was to charge her with all the rage she had ever collected at once. Jamie would fire the gun, and Jess would die in front of her daughter.

And that will be her first memory. Stay calm.

"Put it down, Jamie."

"You left me."

"No, Jamie." Her rage boiled over and started flowing out of her eyes. "You were my best friend. You left to join a cult. You left us. Where were you when I needed someone to talk to about Kevin. Where were you when any of us needed you? We need you now. You just wanted to ignore what happened. We didn't put you away. You did that to yourself. You were our friend."

"I'm his champion."

"Who is he?"

"He is king," Jamie said. She pointed the gun at the roof. "He is god, and I am his champion. He will provide."

"Jamie, is that why you took her? Because of the thing that lives here?"

"He lives in the house. The carnival house."

"What carnival?"

"Sit," Jamie said.

"Momma?"

"Be quiet, baby," Jess said. She inched over, putting herself between the lantern on the floor and Jamie. "Just don't talk right now okay, baby?"

"I said sit."

"Momma," Dominique whined.

"Not your mom anymore."

"Yes huh!"

"Tell her," Jamie said. Jess didn't move, and Jamie fired the revolved over her head. Dominique clapped her hands over her eyes. "Tell her you're not her mom anymore."

"I'm not your mom." Jess's fingers felt for the handle of the lantern.

Dominique started crying. "Momma!"

"She's god's now."

Jess's eyes burned with fury. The heat swelled inside her. She closed them tightly. The burn subsided briefly.

"No," Dominique said. "Momma's!"

"She belongs to god." Jamie pointed the gun down at the stroller. "Say it."

Jess shrieked. Her finger latched onto the handle of the lantern behind her. She sent it flying across the room. It connected with Jamie's head and burning oil rained down around her. It dripped on the plastic cover of the stroller. Jamie was engulfed in flames. She dropped the gun and beat at the flames on her face and clothes. She ran into the hurricane screaming.

Jess ran to her daughter and pulled her from the stroller. Tears poured from her eyes. "Dommy, I'm so sorry." She squeezed Dominique to her chest. Dominique cried harder.

"My mommy!"

"I know, I know," Jess said. She pulled away to look Dominique in the eye. "That was just something I had to say to make you safe. I will always be your mommy. I will always love you. I promise. Do you believe me?"

Dominique sniffed and wiped at her eyes. "Promise?"

"I promise with all my heart. I love you more than anything."

"More than daddy?"

"Twice as much." Jess smiled.

Dominique giggled. The weight of the tears lifted from her heart. She hugged Jess's neck. "I love you, mommy."

The small fires lit the room just enough to see the gun on the floor. She picked it up and checked the cylinder. It had rusted shut. She heard something outside and pointed the revolver out the door. She smelled burning flesh. Lightning struck, revealing Jamie's silhouette standing on the porch. Thunder rumbled, matching her pounding footsteps. Jess fired the revolver. Jamie's head snapped back, and her burning body fell to the floor.

The gun fired again. Dominique covered her ears.

Jamie's body twitched one last time.

Jess pulled the trigger one last time, but the rust wouldn't let it shoot. The bullet exploded in the gun, sending rusty pieces in all directions. The cylinder broke off and caught Jess on the bridge of her nose. She fell back and hit her head on the stairs. She fell unconscious.

Dominique giggled. "Mommy."

26

Totem

The totem stood in the middle of the circles like a wolf tree in the center of a forest it had conquered. It was stained a dark maroon from whatever had happened here before. Streaks of what Eddie assumed was blood had dried like wax as gravity pulled it to the ground. There was no life in this chamber, it all belonged to the totem. The shape stepped into the light of the lantern. It wore a black cloak and glowed with a green aura. Eddie had seen this exact thing at the end of the maze in the haunted house at Johnny D's Carnival Funland. A gold tooth shimmered in the flame. It removed the hood revealing gray and black dreaded hair, and a face that was too thin to be alive. The cloak fell to the ground; underneath there was a dirty suit. The smell of death filled the chamber. At the snap of a finger, flames sparked up from the carved-out circles in the stony ground. It illuminated the chamber and Eddie saw the face of Baron Samedi maniacally smiling. Samedi walked through the flames to the totem, unharmed.

"You ain't think this was over," Baron said. "All cause you got rid of a ghost, huh?"

Carlos pulled himself to his feet. "Honestly, yeah. Cause I'da recognized you."

"Ah, the father," Baron Samedi said with a tone of discovery. "So rarely does the family attend the sacrifice. And even rarer that they would come here under their own power."

"You can't have her, you dirty fuck," Carlos said. "She's not even coming down here."

"You believe so?" Samedi said. "My champion is bringing the child to me now."

Carlos, having no knowledge of a champion or how easily it would be to telegraph a message to kill his daughter, fell silent. He scanned the room looking for some way to defeat this thing. "Eddie, what do you know?" he whispered.

"I'm scared."

"About him?" Carlos amended. "Weaknesses, flaws, anything we can take advantage of?"

"He's a drunk."

"Okay," Carlos said, defeated. They had nothing to drink so it was a matter of what the two of them could figure out before Baron Samedi killed them. Or his child. "Let me know if you think of something. I'm fresh out of ideas."

From somewhere deeper in the darkness, Eddie heard the stirrings of a chant. "Burn them all! Burn them all!"

Baron Samedi raised a palm to the ceiling. The ground broke open and out of it climbed another of the tentacled children. Tentacles dangled from its mouth. It swung its arm. Eddie ducked, and the limb struck Carlos in the chest. He flew back into the wall, dropping his lantern. A smaller fire pooled in the spilled lantern oil. Eddie's mind turned like machinery. He made for the lantern. As he did, a pitchfork banged on the stone floor in front of him. Sparks flashed from the impact.

"Burn them all! Burn them all!"

I'm trying to. Eddie thought. He reached the lantern and had enough time to set it on its base before something wrapped around his leg. It jerked him backwards toward the flames. It lifted him up and slammed him on the ground.

"Eddie!" Carlos groaned. He saw the crowbar and crawled to it. His fingers felt the cold metal and latched on. Carlos struggled to his feet and faced the tentacled child. He hobbled as quickly as he could to the thing, rearing back the crowbar. The thing dropped Eddie. He scrambled away from it. Carlos swung the crowbar. It sank into the child's eye socket. It shrieked and swung a long arm at Carlos, sending him flying back into the wall. More ribs cracked, and Carlos felt them individually.

Eddie picked up the lantern, wielding it like a shield against darkness.

"Throw it, Eddie!" Carlos cheered. "End this fucking thing."

Eddie launched the flaming lantern over the flames at the voodoo specter. For once in his life it came to Eddie's physical ability, and Eddie showed up. The lantern descended on Samedi, but instead of landing on him, it went through him, breaking open on the stony floor behind him, sparking up new flames. Samedi laughed heartily from his gut.

"Burn them all! Burn them all!"

The mob could be seen now. The moment like an amoeba in the darkness.

What did I do wrong? Eddie demanded of himself. *There must be some way to burn it.*

He scanned the chamber. Carlos writhed in pain against the wall, probably dying. The tentacled child pulling on the crowbar, twitching as the last of its existence spun out of control. Samedi laughing, looking not *entirely* there. Eddie could see the wall behind him, the way the flames reached up it.

He's not there. And if he's not there, what's left to burn?

His eyes finally met the totem again. Samedi saw this realization. The laughing stopped.

"End this," he told the mob. The rednecks charged.

Eddie sprinted into the fire.

Beat them. Beat the rednecks, and this all ends.

Torches and pitchforks flew at him. He avoided them all. Eddie jumped through the second circle of fire. He could see the rednecks cleared now, but he kept running. He leapt toward the wooden statue of Baron Samedi, feet first, and with all he could muster, he kicked the totem into the blazing fire. The flames accepted this sacrifice and swallowed the wood. The rednecks rained down on Eddie, but as they drew their pistols and knives from their pockets and waistbands, they turned to ash. Baron Samedi reached for him, his fingers turned to ash, then his arm.

"You think this is over?" he said in his thick Cajun accent. "I don't need your child—I can get any child—but I'm coming back for her. And I'm coming back for you."

Baron Samedi fell to the ground in a pile of smoke and ash. The totem smoked as the fire took it. Smoke filled the room and burned Eddie's eyes.

Time to go, Eddie, he told himself.

Above him, Dominique's voice pleaded for her mother to wake up.

27

Escape

"Carlos," Eddie said. He knelt beside Carlos's weak, unmoving body. "Get up. It's over. He's gone, and we must get out of here. You're going to die of smoke inhalation, and I don't have the social prowess to be able to tell Jess and your daughter without coming off as uncaring."

Carlos examined Eddie's face. He had no idea if he was being serious, but he tried to get up. The chamber filled with smoke. Carlos was blindsided by the thought some monster swinging Dominique by her feet from a screen of smoke.

"Daddy!" Dominique called. Her voice bounced around the chamber.

"Dommy!" Carlos used Eddie to clamber to his feet. He steadied himself looking for the stairs. "Where are you, baby?"

"Daddy, I'm hot. Mommy won't get up!"

"This way," Eddie said. "I can hear her."

"Dommy," Carlos called. "Keep talking dear. I'm trying to find you." This wasn't totally true. He had found her, but he thought if she stopped talking, he would succumb to the pain in his ribs and actually die of smoke inhalation like Eddie said. He had to escape this house. The thing that he had been trapped in since he was a teenager. He and Eddie ascended the stairs.

"Daddy?"

"I'm downstairs." Carlos used the narrow walls to stable himself. The last thing he wanted to do is tumbled back down the stairs over Eddie.

"Stairs?"

"That's okay, baby. Daddy's going to come to you, and we're going to get out of here."

"Mommy won't wake up."

"That's fine," Carlos said weakly. "I'll carry her back to the car."

"But…"

"What is it, Dommy?"

"Carry me."

"This is really fun to listen to," Eddie whispered.

"I'll carry both of you if you want."

"Daddy?"

"Yes?"

"Mommy loves me more than you."

Eddie laughed.

"No," Carlos said dramatically. "Do you believe her?"

"She said."

Eventually he and Eddie climbed out of the fireplace. Smoke had filled the room, but Dominique was small, and Jess lay on the ground with a bruise forming on her face.

The mangled metal of Juarez's revolver lay in scattered pieces around the living room.

Dominique bounced to her daddy, hugging him around the waist. Carlos winced at the pain, but he accepted it as the best thing in the world.

"Can we please leave," Eddie said.

"Yeah, Ed," Carlos said. "Let's forget this place forever."

Eddie helped Carlos get Jess to her feet. Dominique rode on his shoulders and Eddie helped him carry Jess through the woods to her car. Hurricane Katrina beat down on the Outback. Eddie drove them as far as his hotel room. After he and Carlos laid Jess on the bed, he readjusted the pewter figure of Baron Samedi and Papa Legba.

The four of them slept through the rest of the hurricane. The Nelson House burned to the ground. The lives that were lost there, burned with it. The smoke never cleared.

28

Tchotchkes

No one believed what had happened. The police refused to file anything but a missing person report for Duke and a warrant for Jamie's arrest. That was fine with Eddie, Carlos, and Jess. They planned a public memorial for Isabella, inviting everyone in town, especially the senior swim classes at the Y. Later they held a private service for Duke. They took a handful of the ashes from the site and spread it in the parking lot of the Rose Colline Chevy.

Carlos took two months to heal but was back to work by September, first clearing roads and rebuilding houses. He was quickly backed up with home repairs for over two years, and Jess hired an assistant for the daycare so she could help him stay on top of his schedule.

Eddie left the pewter statue on a shelf in a hole-in-the-wall shoppe in the avenues of New Orleans that appeared to be a great resource for tchotchkes and voodoo-based, decorative knickknacks. He left without saying anything. He was back at work before the power returned to the station.

Rose Colline rebuilt as quickly as any other city in the area. Everything was back to normal relatively quickly, except for one thing. The smoke never seemed to clear. Even on sunny days, there was a grayish filter over the city. No one seems to realize that even though the Nelson House was gone, its remains hang all around them like a net.

The power returned and the first business open was Johnny D's Carnival Funland. Its most popular attraction became the haunted house, where the thing at the end laughs when it scared the kids.

29

Something in the Smoke

Rose Colline sat in smoke. Fireman and police tracked the source of the smoke to the woods on the way out of town by the Mexican restaurant that used to be a Pizza Hut. Some days it's clear, and on the days when visibility goes below a mile out, the police and firefighters return to the woods, looking for the source. The clearing in the woods where the Nelson House stood produced more smoke than ever. The King was strong again. The city of Rose Colline and its people stayed quiet. They couldn't see and that took away a lot of desire to be away from home. No one explicitly said it, but everyone knew, something needed to be done about the smoke. Even Johnny D's Carnival Funland was closed, and no one in town had ever seen that. Schools closed. Businesses closed, and only a few cop cars patrolled the streets. There was something in the smoke, and it was going to destroy Rose Colline.

About the Author

Josh Stricklin is an American author and musician with degrees in English literature and advertising from the University of Southern Mississippi. *Katrina* is his fourth terrifying novel with Silver Leaf Books. He's currently hard at work continuing his first series.

CPSIA information can be obtained
at www.ICGtesting.com
Printed in the USA
LVHW111250101122
732762LV00005B/220

9 781609 752934